FOX WAITED . . .

Then suddenly the six pounders banged from aboard the *Minion*. Quickly the sounds melded into one rippling roar as she fired her starboard carronades. Eight thirty-two pounder carronades, double-shotted and with grape shoved down on top, burst into a staggering uproar after the silence.

Gouts of fire lit the scene. Fox, crouching in the shadows of the cliff, could see the outline of the fort, the flagstaff, the checkered light through the embrasures, and the luridly reflected glare off *Minion* in the background. All hell broke loose.

The powder kegs they had piled at the gate blew up in grand style. Before the last of the debris had fallen, before the smoke had cleared, with the massive ringing of the eruption still in his ears, George Abercrombie Fox yelled and sprang forward through the shattered gateway.

Hell, indeed, had broken loose. And the devil himself rushed in with Fox!

The Fox Series

FOX: BOARDERS AWAY
BY ADAM HARDY

PINNACLE BOOKS • NEW YORK CITY

This is a work of fiction. All the characters and events portrayed in this book are fictional, and any resemblance to real people or incidents is purely coincidental.

FOX: BOARDERS AWAY!

Copyright © 1975 by Adam Hardy

A Pinnacle Books edition, published by special arrangement with New English Library Limited.

ISBN: 0-523-00729-9

First printing, October 1975

Cover illustration by Michael Turner

Printed in the United States of America

PINNACLE BOOKS, INC.
275 Madison Avenue
New York, N.Y. 10016

BOARDERS AWAY

CHAPTER ONE

COMMANDER FOX slapped the telescope shut with a gesture of decision and jumped energetically from the ratlines to the quarterdeck of his command. His Britannic Majesty's gunbrig *Minion* rode the grey-green swells with an easy rhythm which Fox was about to interrupt.

"Mr. Guy! We will go down to the Frenchman and put the fear of God into him. Mr. Watson, I'd be obliged if you will put a man in the chains. Mr. Blythe, I'll trouble you to unmask the starboard battery."

"Aye aye, sir," came the three answering voices.

Over there the coast of unhappy France, trembling in the grip of this mad Corsican bandit, General Bonaparte, lay close enough to make life interesting; but not close enough to afford comfort and shelter to the foolish master of the French coaster. He had strayed just a little too far from the safe channels of the coasting trade and the harbours and headlands protected by batteries of the French Artillery and their furnaces heating up red-hot shot.

Fox did not rub his hands in satisfaction.

But he did not deny that a juicy little prize, this early in this fresh commission of *Minion*, would not come amiss. No, bigod! It'd come as an almighty pleasant present.

1

Minion skidded away with the wind, acting perfectly her character as that diabolical rice pudding skating on ice. She was as weatherly as a stout washerwoman in a blow on the Hard; but she had served Fox nobly in the Roulet and she was back off a hostile shore to serve again.

"No sign of life aboard her, sir," observed Grey. He had carried out his orders and now *Minion* swung in to converge with the French coaster. Lieutenant Lionel Grey once more peered through his telescope, his reckless and deucedly handsome face composed as he moved with the motion of the vessel. "Her rags are in a sorry state."

Fox had noticed that disarray of the coaster's sails. What interested him more was the fact she rode low in the water. Whatever she carried, there was a lot of it. She might carry anything: grain, perhaps, timber, meat or hides; perhaps, if the gods smiled, she carried munitions of war. In any case, whatever weighed down her hold would soon belong to the British—to *Minion*'s crew, to her commander, and to his commander, and to the admiral. Fox swore in his customary way whenever he thought of the crosses he had to bear in the way of those set in authority over him. But as of this very minute he was far more interested in so tempting a prize.

The boarding party stood ready. Grey would lead them. As the captain of the vessel, Fox must accustom himself to the idea that he would no longer personally be leading boarding parties, of course, he thought it of especial necessity.

The two vessels were now near enough for Fox to make out the details of the other's deck.

He could see no one, and the vessel's tiller swung idly. He frowned.

There had been no boat rowed to the coast as the

2

British vessel approached. Had there been Fox would have been much more concerned. It was the habit of many French coaster crews when caught by an English man-of-war to scuttle the ship and then row for the shore.

Nothing like that could have happened this time.

Still it was, as Lionel Grey said, aloud: "Deucedly odd!"

They had run through a belt of fog earlier, and Fox had spent some pleasant moments calculating their position and the bearings of the familiar rocks and shoals and treacherous currents of the French shore, not to mention the sites of French batteries. Then, when they had cleared the fog, this luscious tidbit of a a coaster had been instantly espied.

Lieutenant Alfred Blythe, the second of the ship, kept glancing aft. His gunners stood ready. Fox fancied they would not be needed. And he fancied, further, that the ferocious assemblage of weaponry mustered by the boarding party would not be necessary, either.

He would on no account take that for the truth. He knew all about crews waiting in hiding until the unwary boarders came inboard. After that there would be a blaze of musketry, pistols would flash, and then a savage rush would clear away those who survived.

"Mr. Grey," he said, and stopped. Need he give this young tearaway any special orders? Grey knew his ways—or some of them—by now. Grey's half-mocking, half-affectionate smile could always infuriate G. A. Fox. To cover himself and to continue the lapsed conversational opening, he went on: "You'll oblige me, Mr. Grey, after you have secured the vessel, if you will ascertain what wine her captain carries."

"Aye aye, sir." Grey did not miss the point. He knew, as every British sea officer knew, that the British

3

seaman must be kept away from strong drink. But the wardroom and the captain's cabin must be provided with the best the purses of their occupants could provide. A case or two of good French wine . . . Now there was an item of prize that would never find its way back to the damned admiral or to the prize court in England.

And, as *Minion* closed the deeply-laden coaster, Fox realised also that that nice point brought up the equally fine—not to say coarse—point that England was fighting for her life. That maniac Bonaparte had had it all his own way. The Navy was stretched until every fibre and sinew creaked. What with damned French privateers—pirates, more like—swarming out to leech on to the lifeblood of British shipping, the Navy had all it could do to hold on. Even one cargo would make a difference in the scales.

Fox estimated the narrowing distance and just hoped this fine cargo coming up would embarrass Bonaparte more than somewhat. More importantly, he hoped it would enrich him sufficiently to recompense him for the colossal—to George Abercrombie Fox—outlay he had spent on *Minion*.

He had eschewed gold leaf. He had invested further sums of money in first-quality powder. He had spent money shrewdly in other directions. He had bought no fresh uniforms and these days, from preference, he habitually wore his old horror of a hat with the sabre cut he'd acquired outside the crumbling smoke-wreathed walls of Acre.

"Bring her up smartly!" he bellowed, a paroxysm of fury further disfiguring his ugly lumpy face as he saw that *Minion* might pass too close. The damned Frenchman held on.

"Put a six pounder visiting card across her bows,

4

Mr. Blythe!" he bellowed in the old style. "Bigod, the bastard's either going to speak up or put up his hands!"

Alfred Blythe swallowed down hard and burst into frantic activity at the forrad six-pounder.

The six-pounder roundshot spumed into the sea half a cable's length ahead of the Frenchman. Still she held on.

Minion wheeled and forged along, outside her, to larboard and windward.

Fox fumed.

He heard Mr. Kilmartin, one of his master's mates, observe to no one in particular that in his opinion all the Frogs were deaf from too much happy-living in their own way.

This just would not do.

"Mr. Blythe!"

"Aye, sir."

He had to phrase this so that he would get the best out of Blythe, who wanted to do well—like the rest of the crew—but who still was tainted with that devil of awkwardness—like the rest of the crew. The spell of refit when the men had been quartered in a receiving ship had done nothing to improve them. Equally, they had served with this black bastard Fox before, and understood that what he said he meant.

"Knock her mast over, Mr. Blythe. Put a bar shot in and shoot straight." Fox, who knew that if Blythe knew his gun he would hit anything at which he aimed, considered. Then he said:

"We'll make it half-a-guinea, Mr. Blythe. You give me half-a-guinea for every shot you fire before you hit the bastard." He heard Grey snicker and ignored him. "And I'll give you double if you hit him within three shots."

That should even things out. This was strictly something he, as a captain, should not do. But Fox felt he knew his man—and knew the men who served under him.

Again Mr. Blythe swallowed.

He had the courage to say: "Aye aye, sir! Done!"

Blythe laid the gun himself.

Fox glared over the confounded coaster that wouldn't heave to when she should have. Didn't the damn fool of a captain know they could blow him out of the water like a child bursts a soapbubble? Maybe the coaster was deserted. Maybe there had been an outbreak of the plague over there. And maybe he, G. A. F., was thinking nonsense. Blythe stepped back. All was ready.

In the event, Alfred Blythe hit the maintopsail with his third shot. As the mass of canvas and spars fluttered down and the men set up a cheer, Fox fastened his evil ice-cold eyes on his second lieutenant.

"That makes us even, I believe, Mr. Blythe."

"Aye aye, sir. All even."

So it had cost neither of them a penny. Fox considered Blythe to have been lucky. The maintopsail had been a large enough target; the luck came in that one of the rotating ends of the bar shot had swiped with sufficient force to crack a spar enough so that wind-pressure could break it through in a yellow splintering.

The coaster flew up into the wind.

She hung for a moment, then her head paid off, and, like a water-fowl with a broken wing, she trailed off miserably downwind.

Fox bellowed orders that brought *Minion* surging around, the spray bursting finely from her forefoot, the wind bellying her canvas, into a position from which the boat's crew might pull across and board with little

6

inconvenience to themselves. As the boat went over the side, Fox cocked an eye aloft.

Up there in the cross-trees sat Able Seaman Landsdowne. Landsdowne, with his cheeky smile and his shock of fair hair and his pugnacious and yet know-all manners, had proved to be a good lookout. He was not, as least not yet, as good a lookout as Wilson, who was reputed to have the best pair of eyes in the fleet. But Landsdowne was learning fast and, considered Fox with the careful attention he gave to every detail of command, one day would be every bit as good as Wilson. A mere good pair of eyes did not make a first class lookout.

If a long-nosed French vessel—a damned corvette or a sloop, for instance—came poking around, then Fox felt some comfort from having Landsdowne up there.

Grey appeared with his old coat on, a damned great cutlass banging at his side from the baldric slung over his shoulder beneath the coat, two Sea Service pistols in his belt, and a smile as wide as the arms of a Portsmouth doxy.

If Grey thought he was going to have all the pleasures of boarding, of jumping first when the cry: "Boarders Away!" went up, then that harum-scarum young man was seriously mistaken.

One of the quarter gunners—Slocum—was speaking quietly to the after carronade captain—Jenkins—in a voice he did not think his captain could hear. Fox listened for a moment, letting the black tide of devilment flow in him.

"Ar!" Slocum was saying in that soft lower-deck whisper employed by the hands when silent discipline was in force. "They's loot over there, Jenkins, you mark my words."

7

"Jist so long as Jem scrags some vino—that's the mark."

"He'll do that all a merry-o, will Jem. I reckon as they's a fair fifteen shillin's worth o' prize money over there."

Fox felt that Socrum was wildly adrift in his estimate of the coaster's cargo. She was deeply laden, surely; but her cargo could be practically worthless in a prize court. And the vessel was a mongrel, worth practically only the wood from which she was built.

The boat pulled away with Grey very upright in the stern sheets. If there *was* a crew aboard the Frenchman stupid enough to resist the smashing power of *Minion*'s thirty-two pounder carronades, and they decided to open fire on the English boat, then the first obvious target would be the dashing young lieutenant seated in the sternsheets.

Fox felt he did not much care for that idea.

Cursing himself for his own weakness, and yet aware that any act now would only help him overcome his fears, he bawled at Mr. Blythe. Mr. Blythe responded, and the fore carronade belched. The shot smacked the sea as the sound continued to echo flatly in the bright morning, and the brown smoke wafted away downwind.

Grey did not turn his head to look back.

Fox wondered if the young rip guessed how that shot had been called forth entirely on his behalf.

Even if he did, the limb of Satan would only laugh, and laying himself horizontal, would dismiss it as just another curious quirk of his tarpaulin commanding officer.

No response came from the coaster, not so much as the glimpse of a head above the bulwarks.

Fox had been for some time aware of the antics of

8

Mr. Midshipman Gruber. The lad quite clearly had wished to go with Grey. Fox was having none of that. By the curious process of manning his vessel, he was still possessed only of one midshipman. And that one was Gruber. As Grey had remarked when Gruber had begun to fill out: "That lad's been christened by a baker." By which colloquialism Grey meant that Gruber's face was luxuriously specked with freckles.

"Mr. Gruber," said Fox without looking around or taking his attention from the boat and the coaster. "Kindly take yourself and a telescope to the fore cross-trees. Lay into the horizon with the glass, Mr. Gruber. No ogling!"

"Aye aye, sir," squeaked Gruber.

These youngsters always seemed to squeak. Whether they were mere ship's boys who might one day aspire to be warrant officers, or whether they were midshipmen who might one day be full admirals, they all squeaked. They tried to punch the words out, as they heard the horny old seamen do, in that gruff 'aye aye, sir' which remained just on the right side of offensive insubordination that a flogging could not be hung on them, and all they did was squeak like mice with the trap squelching down on them.

Fox banished the squeaks of lads from his mind and looked carefully at the coaster. Yes. Not only was it perfectly plain she was empty of life, but a new and ugly factor intruded.

As he realised this Fox saw Grey, on the deck of the coaster, his pistol drawn and levelled in his left hand, urging his men on. They ran nimbly about the vessel. Presently Grey waved his arms and the men vanished below. Fox watched.

A muffled explosion at his side heralded Mr. Watson, the master, exclaiming: "My God, sir! She's sinking."

"Yes, Mr. Watson."

The coaster sagged lower in the water. The sun shone, the breeze blew fairly, a few high clouds gambolled, and the sea sparkled. But, in all this fair picture, the coaster was doomed.

In the last few moments Fox saw the true explanation of her lowness in the water. She was not laden with booty; she was not filled with good things to loot. She was filled with sea water.

That explained why she was deserted. She had been holed enough to let her fill. Probably her bottom had been ripped on a treacherous rock during the recent fog. This would explain her appearance here, so far from shore. She had been abandoned by her crew as she settled down and the wind had driven her on, a ghost ship. Now, as was often the way with some cargoes, the end of buoyancy had been reached, the cargo was soaked, and the vessel was about to make her final plunge to the bottom.

Lionel Grey and his men remained below.

Fox guessed that Grey must know she was going. They'd see the water swilling about in there.

And George Abercrombie Fox knew what Lionel Grey was up to down in the captain's cabin and store room. The lazaret had probably still been locked. Grey would quickly have that bashed open and—yes! There came Jones Three out on to the deck bearing a case filled with familiar shapes. Jones Three was followed by other seamen, all bearing crates.

Fox began to feel a devilish prickling in his left eyeball.

Grey knew what he was doing. The coaster lurched

lower. When she went she'd go with a bang. If Grey was sucked down with her . . .

What was keeping the young idiot?

Couldn't he feel the vessel under him, her sluggishness, the heaviness of her movements, the rate of roll? Of course he could feel all these things and know what they portended; but, being a reckless harum-scarum imp of Satan, Mr. Grey was salvaging as many straw-packed bottles of wine in their crates as he could. Trust Fox to say something that would run Grey heading into trouble.

Now why couldn't he have remained his normal self, the hard, taciturn, blue-nosed devil of a skipper who wouldn't give his officers the time of day? He refused to use that cover employed by so many tongue-tied captains, and blurt out a harrumph when he had other things on his mind. Perhaps it might be a useful disguise to adopt, to say harrumph when he meant to say something else. Maybe these dim-witted captains weren't so dim-witted after all.

A shrill yell racketted from the fore cross trees.

For an instant Fox thought Gruber was hailing to advise him of the arrival of the Brest squadron, with Bonaparte in the leading three-decker. Then he picked out what Gruber was yelling.

"Ahoy, Mr. Grey! Mr. Grey! She's sinking, sir!"

Now other voices joined the chorus. Even Mr. Watson started in a-yelling.

Fox stuck his hands up into the small of his back and jutted out that arrogant beaked nose of his, and stalked away up and down his ridiculous quarterdeck.

When he got back to the bulwarks again he saw that Grey had appeared.

The lieutenant looked perfectly composed, quite un-

11

flustered. He carried two bottles, one under each arm, that brought a glint to the eye of all the beholders.

As though in rehearsal for the time when he was Admiral of the Red, Grey stepped down into the waiting boat and the bowman pushed off.

His men picked up the stroke and the boat danced over the sparkling water. Fox felt the wind cold on his cheek.

At that, the boat only just cleared the washing, grey-green white ring of foam that burst up where the coaster sank.

CHAPTER TWO

"YOU'VE been a devilish long time rejoining, Commander Fox!"

"Yes, sir," said Fox. His face felt as though old Molly Bright had dipped it into her bucket of starch. He saw Lord Lymm's face give that curious muscular contraction, a kind of convulsive rictus, and with a hurriedness he deplored but recognised as inevitable, Fox added: "I beg your pardon, my lord."

He had made the same mistake when he'd returned from that passage of arms up the Goulet, where *Minion* had towed *Darter* out, and fought a forty-four frigate and a dozen rascally gunboats, and a battery of thirty-sixes that should have been destroyed. He's stepped aboard Captain Lord Lymm's thirty-two gun frigate, *Meteor,* and had begun calling Lymm 'sir' in the normal way any serving officer addressed another. Lymm had gone livid. He remembered Fox, that was quite clear. When the blood rushed back to his leaden-hued cheeks, he'd said in that hateful voice: "You will address me as "my lord" Commander Fox. Is that clear?"

And then, as now, all Fox could say was: "Aye aye, my lord."

Most men with a title had the decency not to parade it about when they went to sea. In that, at the least, they showed some recognition that a title meant noth-

13

ing when the wind howled and the sea roared. Only when you'd become an admiral could you, in all decency, expect your title to be used. No one grudged for a fraction of a second the 'my lord' rendered to Lord Nelson.

Now Lord Lymm glared down on Fox with the gloating expectancy of a weasel inspecting a rabbit with a view to dinner.

Lymm had filled out since the time he had been the honourable Charles Beckworth, before his father died and so, without an effort on Lymm's behalf, become the next holder of the title. His face showed the thick and veinous results of too much brandy, too many lamb chops for breakfast and too much port. His eyes were pouched in that bruised look that told of a man in poor physical shape. With a typically cynical Foxey rush of understanding, George Abercrombie guessed that Lymm had been living it up as one of those sea captains whose ships seemed almost miraculously to be posted to service in the lower reaches of the Thames or Medway. A fast fly could get them up to the hot spots of London in a few hours. Just why Captain Lymm's *Meteor* had been selected to replace Captain Dawson's *Boadicea,* a relief profoundly displeasing to Fox, a lowly commander like himself would not be privileged to know. But Fox knew well enough that Lord Lymm had hated the posting, and would take his spite and resentment out on those poor devils set under him.

The last time Fox had seen this pompous and vicious bastard had been on the blood-soaked deck of *Narcissus,* when mainly through the efforts of Fox himself the frigate had been retaken from the French. That mad night of action beneath the iron guns of the Fort they'd cut out *Narcissus* from Ancre roadstead. Lymm had let her be taken by the French. Fox just didn't worry his

14

head over the kind of justice that allowed the incompetent nincompoop to be given a fresh command. Now, by one of the quirks of Naval service, John Carker was serving as the third of *Narcissus*.

Now if only the good Carter were here, now, and Fox commanded this smart top-line thirty-two gun frigate! As he stood there, lumpy, unlovely, filled with the animal power of natural command, G. A. Fox felt a ghost of amusement over the way in which John Carker, with a whole week's seniority over Lionel Grey, must supersede him as the first lieutenant. He guessed Grey would feel disappointed, despite all that dashing young man's protestations; but, equally, he knew that Grey would give selfless and devoted loyalty. Just at that moment, as he stood in *Meteor*'s great cabin to receive a dressing down, Fox could savour the feelings of a good command with two good men like Carker and Grey.

Then he could no longer avoid the lashing words of Lord Lymm.

"Late, sir! Late. And this miserable tale of a coaster that sank."

Fox was too wise a hand to say: 'Do you question my report, my lord?'

That way lay a quick trip to the chopping block.

"The coaster was sinking when we apprehended her, my lord. We could do nothing."

"Nothing. I agree. Doing nothing suits you most admirably, Commander Fox."

No, there was no doubt about it. This vicious puppy remembered those old days in *Duchess*. Lord Lymm had been the first lieutenant, and Fox the second, under Captain Sir Grantley Struthers. There had been the usual tacit understanding that Fox ran the ship. Fox had met Lord Lymm's present first lieutenant, Mr.

Curwen. Tobias Curwen was a seaman, a mahogany framed hard-case, a lieutenant who knew he had been appointed first to wet-nurse a captain who held his posting only through Influence. Well, Fox might not care overmuch for Lieutenant Tobias Curwen; but he could not fault the man. Had he not been doing exactly the same job with Percy Staunton, the captain of his last ship? Curwen, because of the nature of the Service and the character of the man, would receive courteous and punctilious politeness from Fox. He knew the breed.

"My lord," Fox said, and kept his voice a low monotone.

"And if you so incompetently allowed a coaster to sink under you, what kind of promise for the future is that?" Lymm's breath came faster these days, and his cheeks now showed a flush of anger that appeared permanent. Fox would not care to serve in his ship. "We are here to interfere with the French coastal trade, Commander Fox. We are to bombard, and take prizes, to harass the enemy at every point. And all you can do is report that a coaster sank whilst you stood by."

Fox was not prepared to argue this. He could not, of course, argue with Lymm.

"It is unfortunate, my lord, that the opportunity for prize money did not come our way."

That was subtly sarcastic enough, and yet a simple statement to which no exception could be taken.

But the Earl of Lymm was the captain, and in a King's ship the captain was Lord God Almighty.

"Prize money, Mr. Fox—" Lymm had had difficulty in recalling that the hated and despised Mr. Fox was now Commander Fox. "Is that all you lower-deck scum think of?"

Fox was as well aware as the next man what these aristocratic bastards thought of lower-deck men like

16

himself who had climbed through the hawse-hole to the quarterdeck. He would not be baited. He might have issued a challenge; but that was forbidden and so Lymm would have him two ways. He could say nothing that would not get him into deeper trouble. He just stood there. Lord Lymm glanced up from where he sat at his ornate desk, the sunlight from the array of stern windows shining refulgently into the luxuriously appointed great cabin. He saw the look in Fox's eyes, and he looked quickly back to his desk.

"Very well, Mr—Commander Fox. Just take a warning from this. I expect absolute obedience from every man of my squadron. We have some sticky business to do. Now get out."

"Aye aye, my lord," said Fox. He went out, silently, walking on the carpets spread upon the painted canvas.

Outside he climbed up on to the gangway. The feel of the breeze on his cheek, the roll of the frigate, the ordered activity, the sights and scents of a live ship about him, brought back a flash of sanity. Much more of that and he might have jumped across the desk and sunk his fist into Beckworth's throat. Into Lord Lymm's throat.

He would never have done that.

Not for himself, was his hand stayed. Fox maintained his family of Foxes by the Thames: his mother, his brothers and sisters, in-laws, aged aunts. He would not jeopardise all that for the fleeting satisfaction of a single blow. One day—one day, when circumstances were right . . . Then . . .

The midshipman at the gangway saw him come out into the sunshine and the scarlet-coated marine sentry stiffened up instinctively. To these people, a commander was a high and lofty rank. Not as high and mighty as a

17

captain, of course. But high enough to make them jump.

His boat was alongside, hooked on. He walked down the gangway. No special side-ropes were rove for him, the white rope covered with red or green baize. He would go down into his boat gripping the old worn and shiny three inch rope a hundred pairs of hands had worn smooth.

Well. One day, he, too, would be a captain. That impossible dream must now be so near as to be smellable. It *must* be. He could smell all the odours of Paradise surrounding that magic word 'captain.' One day, that, too would be his.

Of course, there was this lout Lord Lymm to contend with.

Even the most simple-minded could see that the captain of *Meteor,* who commanded this tiny squadron of gunbrigs, with a single sloop to assist, would do everything he could to make life a hell for Commander Fox. Lymm would place every obstacle in his way. If Fox ever managed to make captain, it would only be against the worst endeavours of Lord Lymm.

As he pulled back to *Minion,* Fox wondered if he would have it any other way.

In the miserable days that followed however Fox considered that he may have been too stiff-necked in his arrogance and pride in imagining that. Because one of the sloops—*Porcupine*—had been withdrawn, leaving only *Prosperity* with the squadron, and because the cutter, *Folly,* had been sent about some business that took her beyond Lymm's reach, all the onerous duties of messenger and lick-spittle fell to Commander Fox's *Minion.*

The other gun-brig in the squadron, *Darter,* had been joined by *Glowworm,* a vessel built to the same

18

specifications as Fox's *Minion*. But *Glowworm* was commanded by Commander Dodson, who had a thumping great three month's seniority over Fox. Lieutenant Forbes of *Darter,* a dour Yorkshireman, had, for some reason incomprehensible to Fox, contrived to remain in Lord Lymm's good books.

So, Fox and *Minion* got the dirty end of the stick.

The power of a captain on the high seas was truly enormous. His authority was horrific. There was no appeal and no redress. Fox must do as he was ordered. Nothing else would suffice.

Minion floundered with her unwieldly lines doing despatch work that was rightfully the prerogative of a saucy cutter. The squadron was based on Saint Paul's Harbour, a likely situation from the strategic point of view, being so close to the French mainland; but its isolation could saw at a man's nerves. The tides with their forty feet rise and fall, and the innumerable masses of abrupt rocks, sharp-fanged and deadly, rising from the sea—they often seemed set all about the islands—afforded ample scope for immense practical application to seamanship. That the islanders spoke a kind of barbaric Norman French did not give a man any sense of comfort, and many a Jack Tar felt that itch between his shoulder blades.

Here *Minion* would more often than any other vessel of Lymm's squadron be sent for fresh vegetables and meat and flour and whatever else of food might be obtained. No hovellers were retained for this task. *Minion* also had to load and unload water casks for the squadron.

Grey said nothing.

He had the knack, or so it seemed to Fox, of knowing a great deal more than he should of his commander's business. Between them, Grey and Carker felt

19

they owned Fox. That was the impression George Abercrombie entertained. As it was, a very great deal of grumbling went on in *Minion,* and Grey in his usual dashing and yet tactful way, contrived to smooth things over. Fox fumed. But, as everyone knew, there was nothing that could be done.

No action was to be had. The year was slipping away. The islands of course possessed a wonderfully mild climate, and the cold weather lay some way off yet. Fox looked forward with grim discomfiture to a winter of beating up and down, of running despatches, of supplying the squadron, and of having no damn fun at all.

He became so disenchanted with his lot that all the diabolical streak of vicious bitterness in him bent itself to just one end.

He must survive.

Continually criticised, continually under scrutiny for the slightest misdemeanour or mistake, Fox carried on.

He carried on with his own vicious brand of determination not to break, and to see Lymm broke and in hell first.

If only he could do well and not get into trouble—and that, in God's truth was the more important item—he felt convinced he must be posted in a year, or perhaps eighteen months.

The men he had inherited from the previous commander had been tensed up, shaky, anxious to do well through fear. Now they knew what kind of maniac they had commanding them, and knew of his quality, they would have shaken down into a fine crew. They trusted Fox. But this morale-sapping busy inactivity depressed them. They had to be chased all the time.

He had been able to pick up a handful of fresh men

20

after the refit, but these newcomers very quickly fell into the same dull apathetic ways of their comrades.

Minion did not become a hell ship, for Fox was continually on the lookout for ingenious items to break the monotony. He could never run a hell ship; for he knew that was not the way to get the best out of a crew. But for all that, *Minion* was fast becoming the anathema of any officer with humane principles and an eye for a battle. Fox's helplessness had never, it seemed to him, been as complete as during those days of coastal work in *Minion*.

Even when he had been a powder monkey in *Hermione* he had managed in his Foxey way to break up the routine and to make some brightness out of the drab days.

This, then, was the price of command.

Sometimes the bleak days were enlivened by a correspondence with a freshly arrived vessel. The anchorage at Saint Paul's Harbour, dominated by an old stone castle built, according to scuttlebutt, by Noah as a practice for the Ark, could safely and conveniently hold as many vessels as might be required for the good of the service. The tides had to be watched. But any man could look up to the beetling crags of the castle, which had been modernised less than fifty years ago and equipped with old forty-two pounders taken out of the lower gun decks of three deckers when they changed to thirty-two pounders. Thus, gazing up, he thought himself deucedly lucky he rode under the protection of these guns and was not called upon to storm the ramparts to spike them.

Into the anchorage one bright and breezy day as *Minion* took on water and fresh vegetables, came a dumpy store ship, bulky and unwieldy, and with her came a sleek and beautiful corvette. This was *Pike,*

21

armed with no less than thirty of the thirty-two pounder carronades. At this vessel Commander Fox stared with something of the avariciousness of a starving child with his nose pressed against a baker's window. *Pike*'s captain was a commander. But he was a commander slated to be posted in the very near future—just as soon as he performed some feat of courage and daring. Where *Pike* would be sent the opportunities would be thick. Fox licked his thin lips and bellowed back into his own command, to see about taking on bags of cabbages.

A boat pulled off from the supply vessel and presently Gruber yelled: "Boat ahoy!"

Grey looked up at the midshipman, and smiled, and sauntered across to take a look.

The boat hooked on and a thin and angular figure, looking like some clever animated toy of jointed wooden limbs, made an awkward leap across the gap. Presently this figure appeared over the side, peering about with the uncertainty and hesitation that marked a landlubber.

Immediately, Fox went below.

If there were things to be done, then it ill behooved him to obtrude the unwelcome presence of the captain. Mr. Grey was quite capable of handling the affairs of this vessel and of ensuring that routine went smoothly. What it behooved Fox to do was think of ways to get himself and his ship's company out of the trap. For a moment a flashing glimpse of pigeon pie falling from the foretop caught his fancy—but Captain Lord Lymm was no mad Captain Tranter.

When at last Grey saw fit to inform him that *Minion* had been blessed with another midshipman, Fox ground down the desire to say: "God help him."

"I'm sure another young rascal will be of great help to you, Mr. Grey. Gruber is shaping up well. At least

Mr. Eckersley will have the benefit of admirable instruction."

"Oh, aye, sir. Mr. Eckersley will be instructed."

Well, lieutenants and captains had gone through the pangs of being midshipmen—even admirals had been midshipmen at one stage, remarkable a thought though that be—and no doubt Mr. Midshipman Eckersley would very quickly discover what he had been let in for.

Thinking of Captain Sir Cuthbert Rowlands, the finest sea officer, captain and gentleman G. A. Fox had ever known, Fox surmised that had he to be a midshipman again, for a space after being a ship's boy, he could do a very great deal worse than learn his trade under Lionel Grey.

"Give him time to find his lugs," said Fox. "And I'll see him. Are our goddammed cabbages all aboard yet?"

"Almost all, sir. We also have some mail for the squadron. It is coming across now."

"Ah!" said Fox. Letters gave a man some kind of grip on life.

Grey eyed his captain with that curious lack of curiosity. No matter what Fox did in his damn-you-to-hell cut-and-thrust way, he felt that he would no longer surprise Mr. Grey. He did not like the thought. He would have to go out of his way to make this young limb of Satan sit up and gasp with surprise again.

His bundle of letters contained the usual sweet and comforting letter from his mother. Susan, the eldest sister who ran the tall, narrow row house by the Thames, also wrote to say that their mother kept well, but had some concern over a tickling cough that should have cleared up. There was also to his pleased surprise a letter from Captain Rupert Colburn of the 43rd congratulating him on his swab. Rupert, who was perhaps the only friend Fox had made apart from his family in far too many years, wrote also that he was in expectation of gaining a majority if only he could find the where-withal. Fox considered. He could spare a little money —not much—for commanding a vessel, even so small and insignificant a craft as *Minion*, demanded expenditure all the time, particularly on this kind of hole-and-corner, coastal work.

Yes, he ought to spare Rupert something. Captain Colburn looked out for Fox's younger brother, Bert, besides being a friend. It might not be enough. But it should help.

He picked up his quill and began to write at once, his quick and vigorous writing scrawling across the paper as though he pulled a whaler against a choppy sea. He was in the act of sanding preparatory to enclosing the order to his agents, Snellgrove and Dupre, when Grey knocked and came in.

"All stowed, sir, ready to get under way."

Another captain might have said: "Excellent, Mr. Grey." Another might have snarled: "You've been a devil of a time about it, sir!"

Fox said: "Thank you, Mr. Grey. I'll come up."

He finished sanding the letter, folded it with the order, and then fetched out a wafer from the plain oaken box. One day, when he was a captain, he might have a walnut wafer box, or a mahogany one. There was no time to seal the thing properly, and it would be going under seal in the government bag, anyway. "Have that sent across to the supply vessel—*Drummond*, ain't she?—and we'll get under way as soon as the boat is back."

"Aye aye, sir."

Grey smiled, saw Fox's arctic eyes on him, killed the smile, and left. Fox knew well enough the boat would

24

carry many more letters than the one he had just written. He wondered if any of those busy scribblers would care that he had held up the vital task of taking out cabbages to the squadron so that they might finish their missives with a few scrawled crosses, and entwined hearts, and flowery phrases.

If they did care, one or the other, that would make no difference to George Abercrombie Fox.

He'd kept the boat merely to take his own letter. He owed Rupert that much. He would write long and leisurely letters to his family when he beat up and down so miserably. And—there were the other letters from his acquaintances of the greater world. Still nothing from Wordy; but a fine fat bulky looking letter that might be a manuscript from Godwin, with an enclosure if he was lucky from Sam—who was beginning to influence the older man's views on God. Fox had felt a thin rictus of his lips at this first news. They'd all be going up to Cumberland soon, if they'd rid themselves of the German bug. Fox had a sudden nostalgic pang. One day the wider world would see that all hung together. Again his lips opened. The world would no doubt say they should all hang together.

He let Grey take *Minion* out. Practice was good for the soul. As for his own soul, that was both encarnadined and sooty black, and he was sailing back to a bastard like Lord Lymm who would run him ragged, and abuse him, and sneer contemptuously at him, calling him scum. There had to come an end to this purgatory. One day, one day, he would receive orders that would burst the clouds asunder to let free the hidden sunshine.

CHAPTER THREE

COMMANDER FOX peered through the mist with both his eyes working very well.

"This damned filth!" grumbled the master. Mr. Watson, it was perfectly clear, did not relish fog. Well, no honest sailorman fancied the stuff when he had a rocky coast somewhere off there in the murk and damned dangerous rocks fanging the sea all about.

The interesting fact was, as Fox well knew, they were not honest sailormen. They were fighting seamen, out to sink, burn, destroy or—and particularly or—capture hostile ships. Fog could be a friend under those circumstances.

Fox wiped the moisture from his eyebrows. His eyes could discern nothing beyond the nearest wreathing coils of mist; but he was pleased they were both functioning. He had been wounded, somewhere, some time, and as a result in moments of stress or passion a devilish circle of purple and black would come dropping down over the sight of his left eye, as it had when he'd been waiting for that young rip Grey to reappear on the deck of the sinking coaster.

Somewhere far-off in the fog a bell tolled mournfully.

Fox became at once orientated.

Grey said: "Ain't that Croix de Firminelle?"

26

Mr. Watson nodded his head vigorously. He was as short as Fox and about half as wide. "Indeed, Mr. Grey, and that is what the bell is, precisely."

Fox forebore to correct his image-making.

Mr. Watson was a fusser. He was an Assistant-Master, a second-master, not being in a ship of sufficient force to warrant a full Master—as, bigod! it did not warrant a captain—and he was no doubt as scrupulously working out his chances of being made master as Fox was of being posted captain.

Minion glided on. Fox felt all the movement of her. Many times in his life he had blessed that eerie seventh sense that could transmit some occult tremor through the soles of his feet, or send a freezing chill into the core of his brain, so that he became aware of shoal water, of dangers, of hidden reefs. The sense had forsaken him in Aboukir Bay when *Culloden* had grounded. But normally it served him well.

"Ease her, Mr. Watson," he said in that prison voice of his.

Watson gave the necessary orders and *Minion* eased a little into the offing. The shape of the shoreline lay etched on Fox's mind. He could see every bay and inlet, every marked shoal and reef, could see the spattering pepper-pot dotting of rocks. *Minion* would be safe. Lord Lymm would get his water and his cabbages—and his letters.

If those letters had not all been signed for, Fox would as lief have flung overboard all those addressed with such humble servility to the Earl of Lymm.

That would have been petty.

Fox considered pettiness to be beneath him; but not beneath Lymm. Ergo—the bastard would not have had his letters. But, that would not be.

"I think the fog's thinning a little, over on the starboard bow," said Grey. "Look, sir, there."

Fox looked where Grey pointed.

The lookout had not hailed.

He was in the fog, for *Minion*'s mast did not rise high enough to clear the top levels.

Presently, like a rabbit out of a hat, the brig sailed freely into bright slanting sunshine. Fox blinked. He looked back. The fog made a distinct wall, rising up from the sea, billowing, coiling. The last time they had run through these waters, at this time of day, a fog had hung about there.

Interesting.

"And we have a breeze," said Watson, rubbing his hands. "Capital, capital, sir!"

Any other man would have said: "Capital, sir, capital."

"Call me the instant you sight the squadron," said Fox, and went below.

His little cabin, the grandest in the brig, cramped and confined him. But he wanted to begin a long letter to Godwin, arguing the case both for and against God. It would pass the time. He knew the charts of these waters now so that he could open that closet-door in his mind and take out the tray and see again everything that his phenomenal memory held. That aristocratic nincompoop Lymm would no doubt find some fresh and unpleasant duty for him as soon as he made his number.

Lieutenant Tobias Curwen, a hard man like Fox, would do nothing to curb his captain's tantrums.

What lay between Curwen's captain, the man to whom he looked for favours, and this unknown tarpaulin commander, lay between them alone and Curwen would wish to keep his own nose clean.

28

Fox didn't blame him for that.

He had written a satisfactory-enough argument and was drawing out the subheads when a knock sounded on his door.

He looked up.

The marine sentry was fairly pushing an ungainly figure into the cabin.

"Go on, young 'un," Fox heard the marine whispering between clenched teeth. "He won't bite you—much!"

Mr. Midshipman Eckersley halted before the desk. There was little enough space, and what with desk and cot and the other impedimenta, the cabin was crowded. Fox looked up.

Eckersley's hands were behind his back. Fox guessed they were locked together, the fingers entwined and furiously writhing.

Fox couldn't smile.

"Well, Mr. Eckersley?"

"Please, sir, the squadron's in sight."

"Is that the message you were given?"

"Yes, sir."

"Didn't Mr. Grey say: 'My compliments to the cap'n, and the squadron's in sight'?"

Eckersley's chin sought to lodge itself over his left shoulder.

"I—I—yes, sir."

"First, then, Mr. Eckersley, repeat the message as it was given to you."

"My compliments to—"

"No, no. Mr. Eckersley" Fox felt the gravity of the occasion. "It is Mr. Grey's compliments you are conveying. Now, begin again."

"Yes, sir. Mr. Grey's compliments and—I mean, sir—and the squadron's in sight."

"Very good, Mr. Eckersley."

"Yes, sir."

"You do understand, Mr. Eckersley, the importance of carrying a message and repeating it exactly? You see, when we are in action, and the guns are firing, it sometimes is a little difficult to hear and think straight. That's when I want to know I can rely on you, Mr. Eckersley. I know I can count on you to tell me exactly what the message is." Fox began to feel the biggest humbug in the fleet, and yet, bigod, the truth of what he was saying was undeniable. "You see, Mr. Eckersley, a wrong message might mean we might not win the battle as quickly as we could. You wouldn't want that, would you?"

"No sir. Of course not, sir!"

"That's settled then. Now, convey my compliments to Mr. Grey and say I will be up directly."

"Yes, sir."

With this Mr. Midshipman Eckersley turned his angular form about, ready to depart. He conveyed to Fox the distinct impression of being a jointed wooden puppet slung on strings, all sharp-edged and spasmic. His face was as thin as the rest of him. But he held his back up, and that pleased Fox. The lad's midshipman's uniform looked to be at least two sizes too big for him. Well, that was only common sense. He would grow into the uniform. It was a common precaution of mothers. Fox just hoped the lad would live to fill out the blue cloth and the white trousers.

"Mr. Eckersley."

Eckersley jumped, thinking he had reached safety and had only to pass through the door to relax, shake all over, and then scamper off to Mr. Grey.

He swung around with his spindly arms and legs jerking.

"Yes, sir?"

"Ah, Mr. Eckersley. You are in the Navy now. You should be proud of that, proud of the Service. In the Navy, Mr. Eckersley, we do not often say, 'Yes, sir'—except over dinner, or privately. What we say Mr. Eckersley, is 'Aye aye, sir.' Do you think you can remember that?"

"Ah—yes,—I mean—aye aye, sir."

"Very good, Mr. Eckersley. Now carry my message to Mr. Grey—and jump to it!"

And with those last few words the old Fox cracked out. Mr. Eckersley jumped and scuttled and ran.

George Abercrombie Fox felt old.

He waited a few moments. Then he picked up his old hat with the sabre cut, ducked his head out of his door, ignoring the marine sentry, who must have heard every word of the nursemaiding process, clapped the hat on his head and went up on to the quarterdeck of his command.

The business of reporting in and of transferring the water and stores took some time. Fox endured the usual scathing comments from Lord Lymm. The quarterdeck of *Meteor,* to an ignorant eye, must look much like any other frigate quarterdeck in the fleet.

Fox knew different.

He could see the tiny details—the tiny betraying details—that told him that this frigate was a hell ship. Lymm was a martinet. He was sadistic. He knew little of the way of ships and the sea; but he liked to have everything around him smart. No doubt when he'd been moored in the lower reaches of the Thames there had been gay parties of ladies, coming down, twirling their parasols, fluttering their skirts and their eyelashes, oohing and aahing at the arcane mysteries of sea lore.

31

And Charles Beckworth, Lord Lymm, would lord it over them, right enough.

Thinking back to the time they had served together in *Duchess*, Fox knew without the shadow of a doubt that Lymm was shy.

In two actions when Fox had been roaring and bellowing and cheering the men on through smoke and grapeshot and the rest of the hell that was a sea action, Lymm had disappeared below. Each time he had a cast iron excuse so court martial had not ensued. He'd a smooth line in self-excuses in times of peril. Fox always tried to see the good in people. In everyone. He was well aware that men are not all black or all white. Sometimes he had to look damned hard. Like that Captain Stone, for example, who was an openly declared enemy, who had had Fox beaten up by his galley's crew, who would do Fox whatever damage he could, instantly and laughing at the opportunity—even in Stone Fox could find laudable qualities.

He supposed Lymm was good to his mistress before he cast her off and took another. Maybe he gave milk to kittens or played with his dog. He held church parade with all the punctilio of the man doing a social function. Maybe there were good points to be found in Lord Lymm.

Fox went on searching for them.

The little toady, Lieutenant Haines, was also aboard. Fox was aware of the criminal association between Lymm and Haines, and also aware that he could do nothing about it that would not rebound unfruitfully for him. He might contrive to expose them, get them caught in the act; but he knew with a dark savagery refined and sharpened by his position in society, that the higher authorities would not thank him. He'd be a marked man, then. G. A. Fox was not foolish enough to

32

jeopardise his own chances in order to injure someone else.

Oh, sure, he'd injure Lymm if he could.

He'd do more than that to the sadistic nincompoop if he could. But he'd choose the time and place that would not betray him and his family of Foxes by the Thames.

"All cleared, sir," said Grey. He touched his hat, there on the scrap of decking they called the quarter-deck of *Minion*. Fox looked overside at the other vessels of the squadron. They moved with a jerky grace, lying on the wind, keeping just out of sight of the shore, with a neat regulation spacing about their formation that told eloquently that Lord Lymm had been unpleasant to the captains.

"Very good, Mr. Grey." And then, because his thoughts had been running in such black grooves, and because Grey was such a fine young officer, Fox added: "Cabbages receive the royal treatment, Mr. Grey?"

"Aye, sir," said Grey. He betrayed not a single flash of surprise at his captain's words or tone.

As soon as he had spoken, Fox was cursing himself for a great blabbermouth. What could Grey, caught like himself in the discipline of the Service, say in truth? Fox had always discouraged petty gabble. Some captains talked all the time to their officers. That wasn't Fox's way. As everyone knew.

Then, feeling something more was required of him, Lionel Grey said: "At least Mr. Swindon has the opportunity to pick out the least rotten ones for *Minion*."

Mr. Swindon was the purser—the assistant purser—and Fox did not overly care for him, not because he was a purser and therefore in an occupation naturally conducive to general enmity; but because he picked his nose when talking and bore the marks of a man shifty and sly and by his frustrated attempts to add up a column of figures incorrectly, gave proof of Fox's intuitions. Pursers bore a heavy cross at sea. By honesty they could remove the cross at a stroke.

A thought struck Fox and, although he did not laugh, he took the point of possible amusement.

By sending *Minion* everywhere on the most diabolical errands, Captain Lord Lymm sought to make the life of her crew a misery. Well, he was succeeding. But, there was the undeniable fact that the vessel had the opportunity to pick over the supplies. That was worth something. Fox would sooner live on rotten cabbage and have a fine superior officer, and together get stuck into Monsieur Jean Crapeau—or, at least, just at the moment, here and now, he thought that. He had the gravest doubts that he would continue to think like that if he was back on living on rotten cabbage. Fox liked to nurse his stomach.

Mr. Midshipman Gruber called out: "Flagship's signalling, sir." Then: "That's our number!"

Grey shouted: "Mr. MacMillan! Boats crew. Cheerly, now!"

"Aye aye, sir," shouted the Boatswain. Immediately a stir began as men tailed on, the boat was swung overside, and the boat's crew ran on deck still making themselves presentable. Fox stared on all this activity impassively. Lymm, with a single hoist of bunting, had caused this.

The shrill of the bos'un's pipes died.

Fox kept his old and battered monstrosity of a hat upon his head. He wore his ordinary comfortable blue undress uniform coat, and he wore white duck trousers. Let Lord Lymm take what offence he might. Fox was in the business of fighting a war, not of parading a quarterdeck ponced up like an aristocratic dandy.

The boat bounced towards *Meteor*. What the hell did Lymm want now? It could only be more trouble.

The trouble turned out to be something that, whilst unexpected, came as a refreshing surprise.

In Lymm's overly ornately furnished aft cabin Fox was greeted by a spare, energetic, thin young man with hazel eyes and a gash of a mouth that parted in genuine pleasure as Fox appeared. The man was dressed in civilian clothes. He advanced, his hand outstretched.

"My dear Commander Fox! It is most pleasant to meet you again!" said the man Fox knew only as spy Roland.

CHAPTER FOUR

A SPY was to be carried to the iron-girt shore of France, to be safely delivered past the sentries, the customs-men, the police, the vessel doing the delivery was to retire without loss—and all in silence and secrecy and subterfuge.

This, clearly, was a mission for which Lord Lymm had no taste whatsoever.

Lymm considered the task not only dangerous, but undignified, not really a gentleman's concern at all.

No gentleman would associate with spies.

The perfect man for this dirty work was Fox. He was scum from the gutter. He would be at home with underhand, treacherous, nasty jobs like this.

All this George Abercrombie Fox saw in a twinkling.

He shook Roland's proffered hand.

"Your servant, sir," he said, in the formula.

"May I offer you my sincere congratulations, Commander Fox, on your thoroughly merited promotion?"

About to commit some flowery phrases of thanks to the atmosphere, Fox was crudely interrupted by Lymm. The noble lord harrumphed, and fiddled with papers on his desk, gained their attention, and said: "There is little time left. I want to get you out of my ship, Mr. ah—" Fox felt the lift of amusement. Roland had not seen fit to enlighten Lord Lymm as to the name he was using. Fox knew enough about spying to know that this secret agent might not be using Roland still. Lymm brisked out: "You'll set this—ah—spy ashore in France, Fox. You've done it before. You remember the time you made a hash of it all, jumping into the water to save some miserable landman? Well, this time, sir, I want no lubberly work from you. This is my ship and this is my squadron, now. I want the job done, Commander Fox, and done well. I want no adverse reports going—"

Here Lymm halted himself. He looked like a large and bristly boar challenging some adversary over a midden.

"Aye aye, sir," said Fox. He turned to Roland. "Would you kindly come aboard my vessel now, sir? The tide will serve for tonight—"

"Tomorrow night, Commander Fox."

"I see."

"But, Commander Fox, I will gladly step aboard your vessel. I find the air does not entirely agree with me here."

Lymm missed the point of that, or ignored it, and the spy smiled with that thin gash of a mouth.

"I have a companion this time, Commander. You will be taking two of us."

"Very good."

Roland's companion was called and entered the cabin from Lymm's ante-room. A single glance told Fox that this second spy was a woman.

Oh, she wore a cocked hat, and a man's coat and breeches and boots. A cloak hung from her shoulders. She wore a pistol stuck down a belt. But Fox's old devil eyes saw the swell beneath the coat, the way the breeches strained over her hips. He had stuffed Jennie Blane into one of his best uniforms, and she'd looked a little like this. Fox reasoned that he was not supposed to notice the second spy was a woman, or, noticing, not required to comment on it.

He managed to manoeuvre both of them out of the cabin by addressing Roland, and so not having to choose between a 'sir' and a 'madam' to his friend.

The woman's face bore the harsh and fanatical marks of someone engaged in a task considered absolutely vital. Her eyes were brown, a darker contrast to Roland's hazel eyes, and her lips were too thin for a woman. But there was about her some inner fire, some spirit that Fox could recognise. Despite her uncompromising looks, she was a woman, there was no mistake about that, none at all.

She was agile enough getting into and out of the boat. And, also, she knew enough to let Fox be the last to enter the boat and the first to leave. She would be the kind of woman who would study hard at whatever she had set her mind to. Fox knew the breed.

"You'll have to shift, Mr. Grey," said Fox. "I'll let our two guests have my cabin. Mr. Blythe, I am sure, will be able to make accommodation for himself."

Grey made a face. Anyone was entitled to express an opinion when times came for shifting accommodation in so small a vessel as this. Provided, of course, the opinion was never so obviously aired that the captain must take notice of it.

"Aye aye, sir," said Grey. "I'll see to it at once."

"It's only for one night."

Grey stood, evidently waiting.

"Yes, Mr. Grey?"

"I'd like to look at the charts as soon as possible, sir. When you give me the landing point and times . . . The tide . . . I'd like to . . ."

Grey's voice trailed off.

A look of so diabolical an evil had flashed over Fox's face that his first lieutenant could not continue.

"What are you maundering on about, Mr. Grey?"

"Why, sir." Grey took a grip on himself, and burst out. "I'm the first lieutenant, sir, so I shall be going!"

"The devil you say, Mr. Grey!"

Grey had the sense to keep quiet. Fox stuck his head down and glared up at Grey. The young rip was right, of course. Fox was the captain. The captain did not go off haring into unknown dangers. He sent a subordinate.

"So you think you're going to get all the fun, is that it, Mr. Grey? You think perhaps I'm past all this, hey?"

"Of course not, sir! Lay me horizontal—ain't I seen you enough times—"

"Well, Mr. Grey!" Fox chopped him off. "I've had a direct order from Captain Lymm—Captain Lord Lymm—to take the spies ashore myself."

"I find that hard to credit, sir. No captain—"

Fox knew what Grey meant. He knew, too, that Grey was unthinkingly voicing the views of any sea officer. But just how much did Grey know of the animosity between Lymm and Fox? In any event, Grey could not be allowed to continue to say what he quite evidently was saying.

"You'll obey my orders, Mr. Grey. I know I can leave *Minion* in your care. I'd never dream of leaving her in the care of someone I don't trust."

He saw the look in Grey's eyes. He heard what he had just said. By God! Wasn't it true? Why did there have to be this fencing around in relationships with Grey? Why couldn't he just come out and say, directly, that he'd trust Grey—and John Carker—before any other damned officers in the whole navy? But he was

Fox, and that wasn't his way. He'd come as close as he could. He was getting maudlin. He'd already invited his officers to dinner, by turn. Soon he'd be sitting drinking with them at night. And that would not do. Bigod, no! Only for a reason would Fox do that kind of popular heroics stuff. Now Grey would do as he was damn well told.

"I—thank you, sir. You may rely on me implicitly."

"I know that, Mr. Grey."

And then, again, Fox realised there was no need to add in his offensive growl any promise as to what would happen if Grey failed him, as he would have added only a short time ago. Command changed a man. No doubt of it.

Command had changed Lord Lymm only to increase his sadism and petty-mindedness. Fox received his written orders from Lymm's secretary, a snuffly man whose brandy-drinking and card-playing had made imperative a sojourn out of England for a man of the cloth. Lymm must relish having an ex-minister of religion as a secretary. The orders confirmed that Fox was to deliver safely ashore the two spies. He would fail at his peril. Although this was no specific order for him to go personally, it was couched in such terms that he felt remarkably confident that at any subsequent court-martial he could substantiate his decision.

He was intrigued by the means whereby Roland and the woman had come aboard *Meteor,* to be informed by the spy that, although that was not Fox's business, the two had come out in a boat from Saint Helier, and Lord Lymm's squadron had been the most convenient.

This Roland, whom Fox had met only the once before, and that briefly, at the time he had been put ashore from *Duchess,* was a sharp man. He had an eye.

He said: "I observed another gunbrig, Commander

40

Fox, whilst we waited for you to return, in Lord Lymm's squadron. When I asked, I was told she was called *Darter*."

"*Darter*," said Fox. "Aye. She was smashed up at the same time we were but taken in hand for repairs sooner."

"I fancy she is smaller than your *Minion*?"

"Yes."

"I see."

And Fox reasoned, this spy Roland did see, too.

They got the charts out and Roland sat in the cabin, at ease, his features hawk-like in the lamp-light, studying them. He pointed out the inlet he thought most suitable. A wide enough passage of water, which the soundings showed to be navigable by *Minion* to a distance of some two miles from the mouth. The channel was called Le Sarpenter. Roland pointed his finger to a cove just short of the first village. Most of the land thereabouts, he said, was flat and muddy, and the agriculture somewhat decayed. The village, Panterre, would have to be avoided by him; but, as he said with a smile, that would be after Commander Fox had discharged his duty.

"I see all that, Mr. Roland. Are you suggesting I take my vessel up Le Sarpenter? I had planned on using a boat—as before."

"A boat, certainly, for the final stage." Roland looked at Fox sharply. He breathed out a comment that Fox did not catch, apart from a few blood-curdling profanities. Then: "Are you not aware that you are to fetch me off again, with two passengers?"

"The Devil!" exclaimed Fox. "I did not, sir."

"Then I have to inform you that the countess and I are to be dropped on the night of the twentieth, and we shall be back to be picked up on the following night."

Roland tapped the chart. "Or, failing that, on the next night. I do not think you need trouble to try again for a third time."

Fox knew what he meant by that.

"So you're going in to fetch off two people. I understand. Very well. *Minion* can perform that task admirably."

"Thank you, Commander Fox. I think we shall get along very well."

There was no answer to that.

During the succeeding hours as the routine of the navy swept everyone aboard along with time-honoured custom, Fox had some time to spend in conversation with Roland. Every warship was always, continuously, never-endingly alive. Even in the darkest of nights there were always inboard noises, a part of the routine, to mingle with the eternal outboard wash of water along the hull, the rattle of the blocks, the creak and groan of timbers, the wind in the rigging. When the watches changed, there was the call of the lookout, the man at the sand-glass and the bell—and as the countess, Roland's fellow spy remarked, somewhat peevishly, to Fox: "Deuce take it, Commander! How's a man supposed to get to sleep in all this confounded hullabaloo?"

Fox felt his thin lips twitch.

Bigod! She dressed herself up as a man and she tried to talk like a man. Well, good for her!

"One gets accustomed to it, countess—" he said.

They were standing on the quarterdeck with the stars above them, the moon hidden in cloud, and the sea drove the brig up and down with a long easy motion. She swung about so suddenly that her shoulder struck Fox in the chest.

He wouldn't apologise to her for her own clumsiness.

"Commander Fox! I caution you to stop your dammed great wabbling tongue from spilling out all over the deck! If you wish to address me, you may call me Jean. Jean! Is that clear?"

She used the masculine French form, Jean for John, and Fox knew that Roland had revealed more than he should have or intended to do when he'd called this Jean the countess.

Still and all, Fox wouldn't let that pass without some riposte.

"Your main course betrays you," he said in his ice-chip voice. "Your tops'l is cut too narrow. And your T'garns'l is quite overpowering."

She stared at him as though he was mad.

Well, he was, of course. Most people were mad in the Royal Navy. But she did not really understand what he was talking about. That was delightfully obvious. She had never before had her figure made the comparative image to set against the canvas on a ship's masts and yards.

Fox's cold and evil eyes regarded her with that level and damn-you-to-hell stare he was perfectly conscious of and in certain circumstances—as now, for instance—chose not to moderate. She did not flush, for she was mature enough and in a line of business sufficient to carry her through that peril. She tried to return his look, and failed, and put a hand to her lips.

"I've heard of you from Roland," she whispered.

"You'd best stuff some cloth into your ears, Jean. You'll need what sleep you can muster. This time tomorrow you'll be running over the sand and mud and hoping to hell Boney ain't after you."

She turned away, sharply, one shoulder shrugged exaggeratedly highly towards him, and took herself off.

43

Fox let himself smile with that thin and evil grimace. He had other problems, quite apart from spies. He was like any other sea officer constrained under certain understood rules of ship-conduct. He might go a-prowling, as he often did; but he would not wish, having fierce memories of his own time on the lower deck, to catch his men at their surreptitious pleasures. Only if discipline and efficiency suffered would he check them. He fancied they knew this, and, too, he fancied they sometimes welcomed his appearances, here in *Minion*. He knew why this was; what to do about it exercised his active mind.

Mr. Harvey, the ship's corporal, was a most unpleasant man. Fox had for the moment left him in possession of his position; to have stripped him with all legal procedure would have been impolitic. He had felt genuine sorrow that Harvey had not got himself killed when *Minion* had fought her battle up the Roulet.

Harvey had once been a Master at Arms, had been broken, and as part of his punishment been sent to a King's ship as a landman. Commander Thompson, the man from whom Fox had inherited *Minion,* had rated Harvey ship's corporal. No warrant rank, yet despite that, a ticklish one. If Fox simply derated him, Harvey would remain viciously cock of the walk still. There had to be a way, short of murdering the bastard, for Fox knew enough of human nature to know that if he talked to Harvey and disciplined him in any way the whole ship would suffer.

Musing thus over this and other problems, Fox saw that his command was in good shape. The men watched him as he passed. He did not see Harvey and guessed the ship's corporal was on his rounds. *Minion* heaved over the swell. Routine continued. On the morrow Fox would take her into the inlet of Le Sarpenter. After that, his plans must work. If they did not he would wind up in some foul French prison.

Or he'd be dead.

CHAPTER FIVE

THE night breathed down on the inlet and on the sand and mud, on the inky water where stars gyrated and fidgeted as the smooth greasy waves broke up their reflections. The night breathed down a close and claustrophobic sense of impending disaster.

Fox had engaged in enough night time expeditions to be unaffected by the omens. He was as well aware as the next sensitive soul of the mournfulness, the eeriness, the very menace exuded by the night and the silent onward progress of the boat, and by the glimmer of stars. But he was a sea officer and therefore could not allow romantic notions of his poetical friends to cloud either his nerves or his judgement.

Hoskins rowed stroke. He had achieved a kind of notoriety as the man who had caught a crab and soaked their new captain as he was pulled out to his new command. For Hoskins, that Fox had done nothing about the incident came as not only a welcome surprise and a great relief, but as a pointer to the kind of man he and his shipmates must deal with.

Forbearance, there, had paid handsome dividends.

In the centre of the boat, huddled on the thwarts, the muffled figure of the countess showed as a dull lump.

Roland sat by Fox. Fox himself held the tiller. In this he trusted himself. For coxwain he had a massive Cor-

46

nishman called Tredowan. Tredowan could sit and glower away to himself. Fox meant no disrespect to the Cornishman's skill. But the inlet was dodgy. *Minion* had dropped the boat just inside the mouth. Here the soggy mud afforded no real foundations for a fort, and the nearest one known to Fox lay a musket shot below the village of Panterre. They would disembark Roland and Jean just below that. That was the plan.

Silence had been ordered.

The map had shown a small track on the western bank of the inlet. Roland had had no hesitation in choosing to be put down there. As he had said: "Better to walk a track no matter how foul than to try to wade through waist-high mud."

Fox simply had to agree. He knew all about mud-larking. Had he not spent many and many a day out on the Thames marshes, using his sling to knock his supper, all croaking, out of the air?

Now he habitually carried a carefully folded black kerchief. Shaken out, neatly triangled, loaded with a leaden bullet or a shaped stone, that innocent kerchief could in George Abercrombie's skilled hands become a deadly weapon.

With muffled oars the boat moved stealthily up the inlet and only the soft chinkle and splash of water from her stem marked her passage.

Certainly, Fox had done this kind of night operation before. Many times. Certainly he knew what to do. But—always, every time he took a boat into a hostile shore, each time, he was aware that this time might be the last. Never were two operations of this kind the same. He remembered when they'd taken the boats in to cut out *Heroise*. That had been the night young Dick Calderwood had been killed. The operation had been to cut out an enemy vessel; but it had begun just like

47

this, the long steady pull through the darkness, the soft chingling sounds of water, the muffled thudding of the oars in the rowlocks. The same stars had shone then. But Dick Calderwood would never see those stars again.

He knew exactly where he was. He could just see the darker edge of the eastern bank against the sky. A few clouds had threatened to obscure the stars early on; but they had cleared. Fox would welcome those clouds when they came to turn into the beaching. At the moment the distant glitter of starlight gave him just enough light to see what he was doing.

He glanced at the huddled shape of the countess. He wondered what she was like in bed. He turned his head and looked westwards, across the inlet, to the darkness shrouding the water and the unseen land. The French were over there, the French were all about, looking and listening for desperate people like himself trying to land. Once again he wondered how the French, as rational a people as any on this God's earth, could be so duped and hoodwinked by this Bonaparte. Mind you, had Fox been in Bonaparte's shoes, he'd probably have done just the same. And he wouldn't have been overly finicky about it, either.

The conceit brought up memories he would prefer not to contemplate. His love affair with the French people and their cities and their land continued, even if he would shoot dead the first Frog who tried to stop him, burn any city that would not do as he said, destroy and plough salt into the furrows of any land that did not acknowledge his authority as a sea officer of England.

The skinny figure in the bows waved jerky arms, and Fox eased the boat further from that dark line of shore.

He'd brought Mr. Midshipman Eckersley, to Gruber's extreme discomfiture. But Eckersley needed to be knocked into shape, and this kind of raffish and desperate knight-errantry was just the sort of medicine the lad needed. Eckersley was fifteen, old to come to sea as a midshipman. Of the two doctrines about the right age to join the navy, Fox could see advantages both ways. If you obtained a decent education and then came to sea you were well set up, broadminded, able to look beyond the immediate concerns of the navy. Also, you might have a useful smattering of mathematics and logarithms and calculus. But Fox still felt all those things could be learned at sea, provided you had a good master, and to get the feel of a ship and the ways of a vessel on the oceans of the world as soon as possible, why that seemed to him the most admirable advantage of all. At ten or eleven, get a lad over the first horrific days at sea, knock some sense into him, then train him up by practical and applied seamanship—that was the way to do it. Eckersley knew less than an eleven year old ship's boy, scuttling on bare feet with his leather cartridge bucket.

Those charts Fox carried in his head showed him the ghostly landmarks as they passed on his larboard. Not that there were many of them. A gentle curve, which Eckersley had signalled, indicated they approached the point at which they must angle across the inlet and so make their landfall on the western bank, If they misjudged it, they could run right up under the guns of the fort. If Fox misjudged it, that was . . .

Naval officers shared a special mental outlook on their profession. They tended to look at problems with an obsession for their own ends. There were methods of taking a small boat into a hostile anchorage, or inlet, ways of doing the job that experience had shown to be those calculated to promote the best chances of success. Fox knew that any sea officer could take a boat up Le

Sarpenter. They could find the spot picked out for the landing. They could do this in silence, in the dark, and they could retreat the way they had come, all in silence, and so regain their ship.

George Abercrombie Fox knew, also, that far too many of the serving sea officers, who would do this efficiently, would hardly think about it in ways that were divorced from professional navy ways. Gallant and courageous sea captains, like Sir Grantley Struthers, were mere blockheads when it came to the higher aspects of tactics, and strategy was for them to be found only in what had always been done, what tradition demanded, what had worked in the past.

Fox moved the tiller gently, the boat eased further from the bend in the shoreline. Presently he held up his hand and Hoskins, at stroke, saw the silent command and rested his oar. The other oars rose from the water, lay parallel, dripping water with a faint tinkling diminuendo. The boat glided on soundlessly.

Was that darker streak ahead merely a muddy bank and a straggle of coarse sea-grasses, a pathway, a few leaning trees? Or could it be the glacis of a fort, with the grinning guns in the stone embrasures further back, so far unseen, ready on the instant to belch fire and iron?

Fox felt the slender tremble through the tiller and knew the boat ran over shoal water.

Her way was coming off nicely. He'd sooner have her hit with a meaty thump than risk the flurry and clamour of back-watering now. The two stars on which he had aimed abruptly occulted.

His instant calculation of subtended angles, of distances and heights, made him feel the relief. The height of the darkness ahead blotting out the stars was the height of the inlet bank—it was not the fort.

The boat grounded with the sliding hiss, that sucking sob, that told him he had pure mud beneath him. Roland stood up. Roland had been landed by Fox once before, and so, Fox surmised, he would know his ways.

Then Roland surprised him.

The spy put his hand on Fox's shoulder, and squeezed.

Then he was picking his way up the boat, rousing the countess and with a couple of hands from forrard to assist them, was going over the side on to the bank. Roland gained the crest. He did not step on to the path immediately. He turned about, looking down, his face a grey blob in the starshot dimness. Fox saw that grey blob split by a large smile and knew that Roland was exaggerating so as to be seen.

Fox took off his hat and waved it.

That should be theatricals enough for the night.

There was no need to pass the order to shove off; Eckersley had been charged with doing just that the moment the two spies were safely ashore.

Fox had time for a momentary wonder about Eckersley. As a man completely intolerant of himself, death-afloat to any ridiculous ideas of himself as hero, of himself as superior, of himself as anything other than a hard-working, hard-cursing, hard-drinking—and hard-wenching when he had the chance—tarpaulin lieutenant, Fox entertained no stupid ideas of self-importance. When he made a mistake his worst critic was G. A. Fox. So, how was Mr. Midshipman Sidney Eckersley seeing himself, now? As some kind of knight-errant?

And then a wonderful thought occurred to Fox.

He did not put up a hand to stroke the gilt swab on his left shoulder. But he was no longer a mere lieutenant. True, he was precious little further along the

51

real road of promotion and power, for all that began when a man was posted; but he *was* a commander.

Sometimes it was hard for Fox to realise that, and at other times it dominated all his waking consciousness.

Eckersley gave the agreed on signal; the bowman—a beefy individual who went by the curious name of Tarpy—shoved off and the boat squished back through the mud and lolloped into the water with a splash altogether too loud for Fox's comfort.

Fox appreciated music, all the way from the bawdiest song imaginable shouted out in a low tap room, through all the different gradations to the magic of Mozart—who had died a mere nine years ago—and these new concertos that were coming out of Vienna, and which he had talked about with those who knew during that fine fancy-free period this year in Tunbridge Wells. His friend Wordy would no doubt be thrown into a frenzy by the poetical beauty of the musical tinkle of water. For Fox, a fighting seaman, the music of that tinkling water filled him with a fury all the more terrible that he could not blast and blind and let rip a volatile stream of invective.

He just glared at the boat's crew.

At the grotesque terror of his face the hands bent to their oars, not daring to look at him again, conscious of the enormity of his rage and baffled by it.

The rage that suffused him and turned his ugly face into the semblance of a bloated gargoyle, with bulging cheeks and bulging eyes, proved absolutely justified.

A hoarse hail reached them from further along the bank, followed almost immediately by a musket shot. Fox marked the flashes. Again a musket roared, followed by the cracking whiplash of two pistols. In the silence that fell after the echoes rolled away Fox listened. He strained those ears of his, hearing a wind

52

soughing through the rushes, the water tinkling and chingling under the counter of the boat, and—hearing voices from the bank roused as if in argument.

He could decipher the local French being used. He just hoped Roland or the countess could imitate that patois. That Fox could mimic any language and accent or dialect he heard was a mere fact of his life, something he accepted as a part of his phenomenal memory. He listened intently, and the boat's crew sat mute.

He heard the same hoarse voice lifted, and this time in anger. Another pistol shot banged.

Then—quite clearly, quite distinctly—Fox heard a woman's voice, shrieking. *"Help! Help!"*

There screeched in that voice a torment, an agony, a shame. That could be the countess who wanted to be called Jean. Equally, it might be some drab the devilish Frogs had put up to yelling to entrap them.

They had not been fired at and the fusillade had spat harmlessly off into the darkness, so Fox guessed the patrol up there had no idea where the boat was. The soldiers would be along the bank in a moment or two, though, searching. He opened his mouth to tell the crew to give way.

"Help! For God's sake—help me!"

Well, that was no affair of G. A. Fox's. Spy Roland and his lady friend had been caught. No splashing of a boat back into the water had betrayed them. The patrol had picked them up too quickly for that. Spy Roland and countess Jean had just not been smart enough.

A sadistic glimpse of the expression that would be on Lord Lymm's face when Fox reported back turned from glee to calculation. If Fox reported this débâcle—who would get the blame?

No genius was needed to work out who would be blamed.

The tantalising project of shifting his swab from his left shoulder to his right abruptly receded.

What a botch!

He had no business gallivanting about ashore. His duty lay with *Minion*. Of course, Grey could look after the lubberly brig. And a woman, screaming for help in the night, and the sound of musketry, and—now—the hoarse and hearty laughter of lecherous soldiery. She'd had damned thin lips. But she was a woman, and she was risking her life to bring down Boney. How could George Abercrombie Fox meekly give the order to pull away and so leave her and Roland to the merciless hands of their captors?

Could he?

Of course he could. Wasn't he G. A. F. the blackest bastard in the Royal Navy?

Serve the aristos right for not having their heads chopped off by Madame la Guillotine back when they should have been.

Of course he could snarl out: "Give way!" and so pull back to the waiting *Minion* and be over the horizon with the rest of the squadron before daylight. Well. He stood up. Grey would have to do that. The orders given him by Lymm, and Lymm's own verbal instructions, stated quite clearly what he had to do. Any captain must receive permission from his superior officer before sleeping out of his ship at night. Well—Fox found the conceit rather nice—he'd be out of his vessel but this night he wouldn't be doing much damned sleeping.

He opened his mouth again, and the orders that cracked out were far different from what his crew expected.

54

"Mr. Eckersley!" He used that conspiratorial whisper that always made the men's backs snap up. "You will take this boat out of the inlet. Tredowan will cox. You will report what has happened to Mr. Grey personally. Give him my compliments, and tell him to act according to the instructions he has already received." That should make Grey sit up and think carefully. There were two messages being sent now, and young Eckersley would never know. "Tell him to return tomorrow night according to plan. Rather, say cap'n's compliments and would he kindly return for us tomorrow night. Is that clear lad?"

"Aye aye, sir, all clear, sir." The squeak was just like the trapped mouse. Fox just hoped the cheese was tasty.

"Say, further, Mr. Eckersley, that I am carrying out Lord Lymm's specific orders to land our passengers. Do you understand that?"

"I—I think so, sir."

"Goddammit, lad! Thinking it is so ain't good enough! Say to Mr. Grey that the cap'n is doing what Lord Lymm ordered! Is that damn well clear?"

"Yes, sir—aye aye, sir!"

"Make it so. Now get back here into the stern-sheets."

As they passed in the boat, Fox growled: "Put her nose in again. Mr. Eckersley and let me disembark. Then get outta here as though your tail was alight! And, remember—silent discipline is still in force."

"Aye aye, sir."

The boat nudged the shore as a flick or two from the oars drove her in. Fox jumped with a squelch into the mud. Before he had turned he heard the boat unglue.

By the time he had turned around she had gone, vanished into the shadows.

G. A. Fox turned his ugly face towards all the excitement.

CHAPTER SIX

Fox padded along in the darkness. He could see tolerably well by starlight. The moon would be up soon so that he would have to double his vigilance. He could hear exceedingly well. The night sounds of the countryside around him formed a familiar and yet strangely remote pattern to a man habitually at sea. He could see a few dim and scattered lights from the village of Panterre ahead. Somewhere between him and the village lay the fort.

A glint of metal on the path drew his eyes.

Well, here was where the struggle had taken place. He picked up a tiny pocket-pistol, a model very similar to the pistol Fox often carried. This was a single barrel job, with the cock and flint most neatly contrived to fit snugly, the pan-cover shaped to be just big enough and no bigger. Fox stowed the little gun—it had been fired—into his tail pocket. Probably it had belonged to the countess who called herself Jean.

For the night's work Fox had chosen to wear his old undress uniform coat, the white edging removed now that he was a commander. He wore a pair of boots— not his best pair, for since he had won money at cards he had been able to afford the luxury of a best pair— and he wore a stout pair of trousers. These hung over the boots. Not the most elegant of rigs, well, he didn't give a damn about that; but more suited to hopping about mudflats than shoes and stockings. As was inevitable, on his head he had jammed that old monstrosity of a hat. Despite all the efforts of Lieutenant Grey— and of Midshipman Grey, bigod,—Fox still clung to the old hat.

He became aware of movement in the rushes over to his starboard bow. He halted. For a person who, as a boy, had stalked Red Indians, and slain 'em with his knife, Fox could move silently enough. He waited, a statue in the night.

Presently he heard a soft slithering footstep on the path; the rushes sighed with rustling sounds not made by the breeze. A shadow moved. Two shadows. Fox's right fist hefted comfortably around the hilt of his cutlass.

Moving with a slow and careful rhythm he sank down so that he was sitting on the path. Now he could see silhouetted against the star-glow the shapes of two people—both wore kerchiefs bound around their heads. He caught no glint of rings in their ears. They stood for a moment—and they were talking. Low-voiced talk, it was true, but still they stood talking.

They had no idea Fox was anywhere near. They thought that after the soldiers had gone dragging their two prisoners the inlet and bank and pathway were empty.

Fox thought. These, he reasoned, must be people who had been waiting for Roland and Jean.

There were ways and ways.

Fox spoke in a voice only just raised enough to carry.

He spoke in his usual impeccable French; but he let a touch of the local patois and intonation, already listened to this night, to creep in.

58

"May Bonaparte fall off his horse and do himself a mischief!"

The reaction was instantaneous.

"Qui va la!"

And: "Merde!"

Fox said: "If you do not instantly explain yourselves to an officer of His Britannic Majesty's Navy, you are dead men."

He let go of his cutlass, pulled out the Sea Service pistol and, using both hands, made the cocking of the piece crackle in the night. No one would mistake that sound.

And, too, if these two monkeys did the wrong thing, he'd shoot 'em. Bigod he would! He'd shoot 'em long before they could take a shot at him.

"M'sieur!" And then, after a quick and breathy conversation, the same voice lifted: "Capitaine! How do we know you are English?"

"If I was French and a Bonapartiste, you two would be dead already! D'you think I don't know what's going on?"

He stood up. Now they could see him in the starlight.

If they so much as twitched the wrong way—if they so much as lifted a pistol—then ... But, as though they could read the boil of thoughts racing through his brain, they moved towards him. They held their hands up, high, above their shoulders.

"M'sieu le Capitaine! You brought M'sieu Roland and M'sieu Jean!"

"Yes."

At once the two pairs of hands lowered. The same man had spoken throughout. Now he stepped up to Fox. Tension still gripped all three, there on the muddy pathway beside the star-speckled inky waters of the inlet; but a kind of trust was being established between them.

"Mon Dieu, Mon Dieu!" said the same man. "The soldiers! They were on the path—we could do nothing—nothing! Poor Roland and Jean! They were taken—you must have heard the shooting—"

"I heard it. And the soldiers have taken 'em into the fort?"

"But yes!"

Fox had no time to feel sorry for Roland and the countess.

He stared at the second figure. It was catching: here was another woman dressed up as a man. Mind you, he could see the expediency of it, and the practicality, too. For a girl to go prancing about in this mud in a long trailing skirt and thus engage on the arduous work entailed in landing spies would be ludicrous. He could see little of her face; but she held herself well.

Now, the girl spoke, in a voice modulated and soft, filled with a hoarse huskiness very pleasing to G. A. Fox.

"M'sieu the Capitaine—the plans have gone wrong. You were to return tomorrow night, were you not, to take away M'sieu and Madame Blanc?"

"I agree the plans have gone wrong," said Fox, "unless you intended to have Roland and Jean caught and shot."

"M'sieu!"

He heard the hurt pain in her voice. The man said, somewhat roughly: "The whole plan is wrong. The Blancs will not arrive until tomorrow. And we are not sure of them. I think you had best return to your ship and come back tomorrow night."

Mind you, considered G. A. F. with that broad understanding of human nature which enabled him to tolerate people when they deserved a thump in the muzzle, mind you, you could see this Frenchman's point. He was French. He was engaged in secret work against Bonaparte and his minions. No wonder he seemed a trifle on edge.

"I cannot return until tomorrow night."

At this the two fell into a swift conversation in which Fox, besides picking their brains, also picked up more of the fancy little ways of speech of these parts.

"I need a place to hide for the daytime tomorrow." Fox interrupted without caring for their feelings. "Then when these Blancs turn up they can be taken off."

This, at the last, seemed a sensible course, and the man grumbled acquiescence. He said his name was Etienne—which, quite clearly, it was not. The girl was to be called Marianne. Fox said: "Call me George."

George Abercrombie Fox might be a humble commander and unknown in his native land; the name of Fox was not completely without notoriety in the land of his country's enemies. There were a number of Frenchmen who remembered with different emotions that mad dog of an Englishman who had blown up the chateau d'Agde. Also, with his name at last being mentioned in the Gazette as the first lieutenant of *Hector* during Cloughton's Action, that name would have come to the notice of the French marine, who took stock of such things.

So—George it would be.

"We must go very quietly past the fort. There is a narrow track. It is hard going; but the way is firm, and far enough inland for those hireling soldiers not to hear us."

"What about the customs?"

"They are everywhere, like lice; they have an office in Panterre. They should not concern us here."

61

"Lead on," said Fox.

If anyone thought he was going to lead a forlorn hope against the fort to rescue Roland and Jean—then that someone didn't know G. A. Fox.

As they marched along, very quietly, not speaking, with the stars a frosty glitter high above them and the first paling hint of the moon rising, Fox recognised the waste of a good man. He'd quite taken to Roland. The man seemed to see things, to see through both men and events that so many other people would have had no idea existed. It was a great pity. And as for the countess—and damn her thin lips—she must be a brave woman. Yes, a great shame.

Just how important these Blancs were, Fox had no way of knowing. Blanc would be a cover name for them, also. Perhaps they carried some secret that would change the course of the war. What Fox did know, and with clarity, was the fact that his orders called on him to land the spies, and to pick them and their passengers up again. He was perfectly within his orders to do what he was doing. Or—this point he would argue with great passion at his court martial.

That the high and mighty big-wigs at home would certainly consider two French spies with important information about the war and, possibly, of Bonaparte's intentions, far more vital to the good of the country than a mere bumpkin commander would in a most satisfyingly inverted way work in his favour.

He plodded on silently.

Now the moon was beginning to appear, a muzzy yellow glow. Ahead of them the lights of Panterre had died now to a couple of widely separated dots of light. The breeze blew. There were crops in these fields, and the distant lines of poplars told of better roads than the track they trod. Autumn would be upon the land soon and the harvesting would begin. Perhaps the bones of Commander Fox would moulder in one of the hedgerows?

With an exaggerated caution that, with his experience, Fox found not ludicrous but highly efficient, the two led him through the sleeping village and to a house, set on the outskirts. The inlet at last narrowed here. A river ran down and burbled beneath an old stone bridge that might have traced its foundations to the Romans. Once inside the house, and with all windows shuttered, a light could be struck, a lantern lit, and they could breathe more easily.

A blast of profanity to ease his feelings appeared to Fox to be inappropriate.

He was given a glass of wine, reasonable stuff, and he decided to get his head down in the bed they showed him.

Marianne threw off her cloak, coming into the room. She gave a quick toss to her head, and her curls fell free from under her kerchief. Fox appraised her. Nice. Very nice. Somewhat broad in the jaws, but with an uptilted-nose, wide blue eyes, and hair of that brown just this side of corngold. She possessed, like so many unfortunate Frenchwomen, the beginnings of a moustache. But, taken all in all, she was very nice.

"You should be safe here, George. Now I must sleep, for there is a great deal to be done on the morrow."

"Thank you, Marianne. I'll expect you tomorrow night, then?"

"Yes."

"You cannot sleep here tonight?"

If it was clumsy, boorish even, Marianne ignored that. Perhaps she had had experience of sailors before. Panterre besides being a fishing village was also used as

a coasting halt. The coasters the British continually
tried to capture would run up the inlet of Le Sarpenter
and lie snugly under the guns of the fort.

Fox's information on the fort said it contained six
thirty-six pounders.

"No, George. I am tired. I need sleep."

"The fort. How many guns are there?"

"Ten. Big ones. And there is a company of soldiers,
also."

Fox filed that away. He couldn't smile. Marianne
took her clothes from a closet and went into the next
room to change. He heard the outside door closing very
softly after a time, and regretted he had not seen her
dressed as a woman.

Etienne came in, yawning, and flopped down on the
other bed without undressing. Fox let his body down,
and felt the blankets, and sheets, and pillow . . . and
then he was blinking his eyes open and morning sunshine was streaming in through the gaps in the shutters.

A heel of bread and a piece of rank cheese, with a
glass of the same wine as he had drunk the previous
night, provided him with breakfast. Fox would survive.
Survival was a matter of adapting. During the day he
sat in a polished wooden chair, propped back against
the wall, his head sunk on his breast. He thought.
There were no books in the house; there were but the
two rooms, with the privy outside against the wall, and
the scope for dredging from his memory whatever took
his fancy could not have been greater. He reviewed
much of his life, did G. A. Fox, and found so much of
it to be drab and unrewarding, shot through with the
scarlet fires of battle and sudden death. He thought of
Sophy, daughter of Lord Kintlesham. Once, in the
Mediterranean, she had been fat and sweaty, a red-
cheeked goose, simpering all over him, declaring he

was her Foxey, her hero. Now she was the Duchess of Bowden—the dowager Duchess, he wondered—slim and elegant, fabulously wealthy, a beauty who had buried two husbands and yet remained a virgin, a cold and icy aloofness in her manner reserved with special intensity for that miserable drunken loud-mouthed loose-living George Abercrombie Fox.

Well, he often thought of Sophy when his mind turned to women.

With the setting of the sun Marianne returned. Fox wouldn't mind tumbling her. But she was all business. Etienne had gone to the rendezvous to fetch the Blancs to this safe house. The moment they arrived the party would set out for the walk from the village, past the fort, out along the path by the inlet. The time would be the same as the previous night. The moon would be up later on; they wanted the business finished by then. The Blancs must be aboard the English ship, Etienne and Marianne must be back to Panterre. Marianne, whose accent faltered at times, as though she merely aped the local dialect in the attempt to fit in, mentioned in a fit of abstraction, when Fox was eyeing her with a particular meanness, that she would have to get back to Paris at once.

"Ah, Paris!" said Fox.

"You have been to Paris, George?"

"Yes. Things were changing fast at the time."

Now it was Marianne's turn to say: "Ah!"

Fox did not enlighten her. Good grief—he'd had a right roaring time of it then, and to tell this girl what had happened would take all night, and more. Mind you, she might be amenable by that time . . .

Marianne saw the look in Fox's eyes, and understood perfectly what this wild sea-wolf of an English captain wanted, had the nerve not to blush, and so said: "I have much work to do in Paris that is of no concern of yours, George. For now, you are merely a porter taking passengers in your ship."

"Right," said Fox, more than a little drily. "I'll remember that."

What he would also remember, and with far more reality than this girl's feeble affectation of command, was the way her breasts moved as she walked, the swing of her hips, the purpose in her face—and that damned moustache.

And that, of course, brought up the unwelcome fact that his own face was like a boar's back of bristle. English sea officers were clean-shaven, and smart with it. He felt the itchiness of his chin and cursed. No one seemed to bother that he looked more like some skulker in the hedgerows, unshaven and gummy-eyed, then a professional fighting sea officer. Then Etienne came in swiftly, his long cloak swirling, his knee-boots splashed with mud, cursing in a way that made all thoughts of shaving seem the flimmery they were.

When the Frenchman had calmed down enough to leave off cussing and tell them what had happened, his news made Marianne squeal in dismay and Fox take up the cussing stakes.

"The Custom house men have taken the Blancs! They're being held for questioning, and their stories won't deceive those professional bloodhounds for half a minute! I came straight here." Etienne hushed Marianne, and Fox shut up to listen.

"It's all over, Marianne!" Etienne was now speaking a French that had grown in Paris, and not in the cabbage fields around Panterre. "We must pack and go, tonight, now! It's finished!"

"You mean," said Fox, and his voice was extraordinarily ugly. "You mean to leave the Blancs in the hands of Boney's men?"

"What else is there to do?"

Whatever there might be to do, of one thing Fox was absolutely sure. If a mess were made of this operation, if the Blancs weren't brought off as his orders called for, then Lymm would have every excuse to chop him. He'd kiss goodbye to shifting his swab's shoulder housings. He'd be the scapegoat, and this time it would be fatal. Fox picked up his cloak.

"Bigod! I'll show you what's to do!" And Fox clapped his monstrosity of a hat on his head and made for the door.

CHAPTER SEVEN

THE night hung infernally dark about his ears, with high cloud cutting off that familiar cold glitter of the stars. He groped his way along the wall. If Etienne and Marianne wouldn't come, he'd damn well go on his own. He had a certain way with him, had G. A. Fox, when it came to dealing with the uniformed lackeys who took Boney's money and did Boney's dirty work for him.

He knew where the customs house was because he'd asked as a mere matter of ordinary precaution. Anyway, it would be near the waterfront, and it would most probably be one of the houses with a light still burning. He was right on both counts.

He stuck his boot into some filth along the street, and cursed and waggled his boot in the air. He moved on again, silently, and he heard the two coming out of the house at his rear and following him. If they'd had to stalk scalp-hunting Red Indians in a ravaged fort, they'd have soon been hairless.

He waited for them. So dark was it that Etienne would have bumped into him, had not Fox growled a low curse and a standoff, damn you!

"You are a madman, George!"

"I know that. I'm not doing this for the whoreson Blancs. Come on, and do exactly as I say."

"Now wait a minute—"

But Fox had gone.

He had made no sound as he moved towards the custom house. The place hung over the water on stilts, with its front door opening on to the road through the village. He could hear horses in stables to the side. Men were laughing and singing in a room to the right of the door and lantern light spilled out from a window only casually shuttered.

Fox went to the door from the opposite direction. He was breathing smoothly and evenly. This was simply a confounded interruption to the plans. How many in there? He listened—difficult to judge. Probably three or four; certainly no more than six. There'd be a lieutenant, probably. A sergeant, too. They must have either finished questioning the Blancs or were saving them for someone of greater authority in the morning.

Fox scowled with his horrific grimace. He would be the someone of greater authority. He took out one of the Sea Service pistols. This was his badge of rank tonight.

With the due genuflection to his accepted mode of behaviour, he checked the other pistol, his cutlass, the seaman's knife at his right hip, and the little hide-away gun he had picked up on the path. This he had loaded with a loose scrap of iron Etienne had found in the house, and with a wad it fitted snugly enough. The two agents came up at his rear, making some noise, but not disturbing the revelry within the custom house. The Blancs would probably be locked in a room at the back, over the water. There was no time to attempt a fancy rescue by cutting through the floorboards from a boat on the river, although the idea was pleasant enough.

Grey or Blythe would be steering the boat up the inlet and Fox had no wish for a boat's crew of *Minion*'s to be hanging around too long. They'd get up to some mischief, for sure.

He went straight into the doorway, seeing the door on his right was closed; the door on his left opened into a shadowy space that he could just make out as an office of some kind. He went on. A light showed ahead. Narrow stairs opened to his left, the passage jinked under them. The door at the end stood half-open, and he could just make out the misshapen shadow of a man sitting in a high-backed wicker watch-chair, leaning forward to take up a glass of wine from a low table. Fox went in so fast the man did not know what struck him. Fox eased him back into the chair with one hand—his right hand holding the pistol—and his left took the glass of wine.

Never one to waste an opportunity for a free drink, Fox tossed the wine back. Better stuff than he'd had at the safe house, that was for sure. The man's head was a mass of blood at the back, matting the hair, and some of that blood stuck greasily to Fox's pistol barrel. He wiped it thoughtfully on the man's blue uniform coat.

The lantern showed him the locked door. The keys hung on a beaten-iron ring. When Fox unlocked the door and eased it open so that light streamed in, he said, softly but in such a cutting whisper that the two people illuminated by the light jumped in shock:

"Not a sound! Come out quietly. You are quite safe, Monsieur, Madame Blanc. But as you value your lives—not a sound!"

They crept out like churchmice visiting town.

With a ferocious roll of his eyeballs, Fox indicated they should precede him down the passageway. The woman saw the man, all slumped and bloody in the chair, and she started in fright, but her husband gripped her around the waist and bore her on, past the closed door where all the singing and laughter emanated from, and they walked out of the front door, free.

Marianne said: "I would not believe it—"

"Shut your trap," said G. A. Fox with urbane politeness.

He drove them on before him, down the street towards the end of the village and the shadows of the pathway by the inlet. Anybody walking about at this hour in France at this time was asking for trouble. Fox kept his eyes peeled.

As soon as they were far enough away to talk a little more freely, Fox whispered: "Just keep on walking, don't make a noise, and you'll be all right. I'm George. That is all you need to know."

"But," said Monsieur Blanc.

"Walk!"

The way Fox spat out that *'Marche!'* made them march like grenadiers along the path. As the moment for passing the fort approached, Fox cautioned them again. This was all going very well. Smoothly. Probably, knowing his typical Foxey luck, it was going too smoothly.

That made him halt and swing around to face Etienne and Marianne. They were mere blurs in the starlight, where the clouds were already moving like dreams and dissipating like hopes.

"You two have your work to do. You have done your job here. You should return to Panterre, ready to leave for Paris in the morning."

Marianne spoke quickly, before Etienne had a chance to open his mouth:

"We will see the Blancs to your boat, George."

"As you will."

Marching on through the night, Fox began to feel

71

more and more dissatisfied, uneasy, itchy. Goddammit to hell! What else could he do? His duty was plain. Get these Blancs out of France and to safety. They were mere lay figures, cardboard cut-out characters, of no interest—at the moment—to him apart from their function as bodies for transportation.

The countess who called herself Jean, and Roland—they were real people. They were flesh and blood, for all that he had known them for so short a time. He appreciated the cool courage of Roland, his perception, his way of speaking. He felt a little pity for the countess's thin lips; but she was a woman, and she had a fire that intrigued.

As he had thought just then—Goddammit to hell!

They skirted the fort by that round-about path. Marianne had said the fort now mounted ten guns. They might all be thirty-sixes; they could as easily now be forty-twos. Marianne had said big ones; she did not know what weight they were. They could be forty-eights. Well, it was obviously no good carrying on this train of thought. He began to look with a certain uneasy eagerness that displeased him for the first sign of the boat as they came back to the path and trod along to the rendezvous point.

Grey had sent Lieutenant Alfred Blythe.

The boat waited, a dark splotch on the sheen of the water.

Well, Grey was perfectly correct.

Grey was now in acting command of *Minion*. He had therefore delegated boat duty to his subordinate. His first duty was to his vessel.

Despite all that, Fox experienced a thrill of dismay that it was not Grey who whispered hoarsely: "Ahoy there! Cap'n?"

"Stow your gab!" Fox whispered in his best cutting

style back. He need not take cognisance that an officer had hailed. It could have been anyone. He went up to the stem of the boat and laid a hard and horny hand on her gunwale. The boat felt good after a day and a night away from the sea.

"Get you aboard," he said to the Blancs. They made a mish-mash of it, and Tarpy the bowman had to help them over and on to seats on the thwarts. Fox turned to Etienne and Marianne.

"You've done your duty," he said. He spoke more harshly than he intended. "Now I must do mine."

"But," said Marianne.

Fox marvelled. She was crying.

"What of Roland—and Jean?"

"One cannot simply walk into a fort crammed with soldiers and release them, as we did with the Blancs. And, anyway, by this time the customs men will know their prisoners have escaped. They will be along soon. So you'd both better be lively."

"But—" said Marianne.

All these confounded buts!

They were enough to drive a man silly.

Fox put his booted foot over the gunwale.

"Goodbye, Etienne. Goodbye, Marianne."

"George—cannot you do *something*?"

The quick reply, the sensible reply to that was: "No!"

But, of course, he could do something.

The only answer a British naval officer acting under orders could give was that final condemning 'no'; but since when had George Abercrombie Fox cared a fig about orders that did not suit his own plans?

Since he had been made commander, perhaps?

These late summer nights were still short. That made him realise his birthday was coming up next month. A fine time to recall that! And yet—didn't it emphasise the whole thing? Didn't it bring home to him that Roland and Jean might have no more birthdays at all?

Of course he could do something, if he disregarded orders he had already bent to his own purposes, and took a typical Foxey cunning and sly attitude to what remained.

"Etienne," Fox said in his harsh and hateful voice. "You will have to scout. If the soldiers have moved Roland and Jean by tomorrow it will be useless. We can do nothing tonight. Tomorrow night—then we might do something."

"George!" said Marianne.

Her voice carried within the breathed word a gasp of thankfulness, so that the sob awoke a stir in Fox's mind. Of course! He had been foolish not to see this before. Roland and Marianne . . . Of course!

"I can find out what the soldiers are doing," said Etienne. "I have a friend who takes wine to the fort. But it is too dangerous for Marianne to stay in Panterre any longer. We should have left first thing in the morning."

"Step aboard, Marianne. And quickly. I don't want my first lieutenant nosing up here after me."

Which, as Fox well knew, was just what Grey would do . . .

And, as his fine careful plans were put together, as he had tested himself—and found himself sadly wanting in naval discipline—as he was preparing to lead a great heroic rescue operation on the morrow, he heard the low and urgent call from Alfred Blythe in the sternsheets.

"There's a vessel coming up the inlet, sir!"

Fox knew.

He'd been thinking what Grey would do—what he would have done in Grey's shoes—and the right roaring imp of Satan had done it! He lumped around and tried to see over the dark water. A shadow moved.

Yes, by God! Grey was bringing *Minion* up Le Sarpenter!

At that moment Fox had no clear idea if he wanted to bawl in so outrageous a fashion at Grey for hazarding his vessel, or to clap him on the back and swear he was the most capital fellow alive. Bigod! What a thing!

"It's *Minion*, sir," offered Blythe.

"Get aboard, Etienne." Fox scrambled back along the boat. "Push off, Tarpy. And no noise, or you'll have a red checked shirt at the gratings tomorrow."

Tarpy nodded and thrust with the bowhook.

The boat sloshed back; the noise was just not sufficient for Fox to have to implement his threat of a flogging, and the hands began to pull out. Grey would see them. The lad had eyes that could spot a pretty ankle at two hundred paces.

The business of getting aboard *Minion* occupied enough time so that Fox was beginning to think he would have to stick to his plans. But here came Grey, his face frozen, clearly not knowing what tack his unpredictable commander was going to take. Fox gave him no time to worry over that score.

"Rouse out everyone, Mr. Grey; but no beating to quarters. Silent discipline! Silent, mind! Pass the word for Sar'nt Dunn to lay aft. I shall give you your orders as we proceed. Have Mr. Smith roused out. We've a lot to do, Mr. Grey, and precious little time to do it in."

"Aye aye, sir."

Grey asked no questions. He carried out what Fox had ordered in his usual impeccable way, the embodiment of efficiency. Fox wondered if, perhaps, Grey might be ruthless enough when it came to command.

But, he had to admit, Grey got things done. That was what counted.

The marine sergeant came aft, scarlet faced, Fox guessed, although in the dimness everything lay shadowed and ghostly, unreal. His scarlet uniform appeared a misty black-grey.

Fox had a lot of time for the Marines.

He gave his orders in language that the sergeant would understand. Fox was as well aware as the next sea officer of the smashing power and moral value of a marine volley at the crucial moment of a battle. Sergeant Dunn nodded to show he understood. Fox sat at his desk in his own cramped little cabin. His four guests were quartered somewhere, and later on he would see to them properly; for now he wanted to work uncluttered. He had Etienne—and Marianne, who also knew the scheme—draw out a sketch-plan of the fort, and Mr. Smith, the gunner, came in and was soon deep in technicalities.

"Not that it'll take much, I think, Mr. Smith, to knock the gate down. But don't skimp. A nice big bang is of capital moral value."

"Aye aye, sir."

Sergeant Dunn had a query about bayonets, which Fox could answer crudely. His coarseness amused the marine sergeant, Fox could see that, but service discipline kept the craggy features of Sergeant Dunn ramrod stiff.

There was some business about the length of match to be employed.

"Cut it short, Mr. Smith! We won't have a lot of time to hang about."

"Aye aye, sir. We'll have a lovely bang."

Fox glanced up. Mr. Smith was a regular warrant officer of the old school, although not an old man, and if

76

he was taking this tone, then perhaps there was more hope for *Minion* than Fox had surmised. Maybe his attitude with the crew was getting through. But now was no time for that. Now was a time for rapid planning, for preparation, and then for action.

"I'll look to you, then, Mr. Smith."

"Aye aye, sir."

There was the moment when the ship's corporal must superintend the issuing of small arms to the crew. Here was a moment of danger. If one of the hands could not wait and simply shot Harvey through the head, or stuck a cutlass through his guts, there and then? Fox prayed they'd wait to knock the whoreson bastard off later on, when it could be decently written down as a casualty of the action.

When his expected difficulty with Mr. Grey came to a head, as he had known it would, he had to act as though Grey's idea had never occurred to him.

Lieutenant Lionel Grey stood at the area of deck that corresponded with what would have been the forward end of the quarterdeck, for *Minion* was flush-decked and possessed no gangways. He turned as Fox came out on deck. Fox sighed.

Mr. Grey wore an old coat. He had his cutlass slung on a baldric under the coat. He had no less than four pistols stuck down his belt at various places. He looked exceedingly fierce.

"I have checked the timing and match with Mr. Smith, sir. The powder is all stowed, ready and dry. We're all ready to leave, sir. I was about to step below to inform you."

Fox, who still wore all his previous gear, stared with stony eyes at his first lieutenant.

"Mr. Grey," he said in that brusque, grating voice. "You were left in temporary command of this vessel.

77

The captain was unavoidably detained ashore carrying out his orders. You are still in temporary command. I am still in fact ashore about the King's business."

"But, sir—" began Grey.

And then, G. A. Fox—the big blabbering mouth of him—could not resist a final dig.

"I shall be leading the shore party, Mr. Grey. What! Did you think you'd do me out of all the fun?"

CHAPTER EIGHT

THAT was not like Fox at all.

Fun?

What! Didn't he know only too well by now what the horror of fighting was like? Didn't he know the blood and the agony, the filth and the stench of it? Why the hell was he sounding like some schoolboy hero, idiotically prating of the fun of battle? Because Etienne was going, and Marianne stood at his side? Was that it?

He'd left Grey with enough men to man the starboard carronades and the sweeps. A few sail trimmers had been left, also, and those not fit to go. The rest he crammed into the two ship's boats and they pulled silently for the cove where they had landed previously.

The boats grounded with that sobbing suck of mud and the men sprang out. The marines under Sergeant Dunn, acting under orders, made no attempt to form up. Everyone moved along the path soundlessly, going one behind the other in Indian file. And in each one of those heads Fox had instilled the terror of his wrath and the horror of what would happen if they made the slightest sound.

So many old slops had been torn up to muffle equipment the purser would have a field day later on.

This kind of skylarking about, creeping stealthily

79

along in enemy countryside, pressing on to attack a fort, this kind of calculated insanity always made the breath come fast in the throat, the heart beat quicker. Fox knew that plenty of those men behind him would have the tremble in their calves, and their fingers would grip their cutlasses or muskets or tomahawks with a more tenacious grasp so as to still the shakes.

As for him, well he'd done this before. It was what he was paid to do. It was a living.

The fort was garrisoned by about a company. Given that Boney was thinning everything down, two hundred men would be an overestimate. There were also the gunners, perhaps another hundred. Huge odds? Oh, yes, huge odds. About three hundred men, or, to be optimistic, two hundred and fifty, against *Minion*'s landing party of sixty. But, then, those of the British navy were so accustomed to fighting huge odds and winning that no thought of defeat could enter their thick heads. Handfuls of men had rushed defences thickly manned with enemy troops, and had carried them. Incredible feats had been performed when English ships had taken French or Spanish ships. Tiny groups of men had overcome large crews. It always seemed the same. So Fox had no qualms about the odds.

He did have qualms about the damned moon.

If she got up before he could get in his first whack, she might betray the enterprise.

He set a cracking pace, marching on the fort, and he listened for any gasps of effort from behind in case his men were not fit. But life at sea gave a man that special brand of fitness and toughness to endure frightful rigours. The hands stumbled on after him. And, he had to admit, all in all, they did not make overmuch noise.

They'd take it in turn to carry the powder kegs.

Mr. Smith marched up with the advance party. Alfred Blythe was there, as were the two midshipmen. He'd taken only one of his three master's mates, and had left the choice to Grey who he would keep. Grey had chosen Longbridge and Kilmartin, thus allowing an excited Mr. Partridge to go with the landing party. Both Kilmartin and Longbridge had looked exceedingly cut up and disgruntled.

Tarpy, the beefy bow oar, trudged on carrying *Minion*'s one and only seven-barrelled musket. Fox knew Tarpy gave the monstrous thing the love and affection a mother bestows on an only child. He cleaned it and cared for it, and made sure it would function perfectly. Fox was rather looking forward to seeing Tarpy in action with the monster.

Tarpy had a Welshman—called Taffy, with great orginality—to help him with the gun, for although, and surprisingly, it weighed only twelve pounds, two men could handle the thing more easily than one. Fox thought of the singular Mr. Chatto, of whom Lord Kintlesham had spoken, and of Mr. Chatto's remarkable inventions and ideas. Privately, Fox had thought that this Mr. Chatto, whose antecedents were as murky as Fox's own, was a shark, and was only out to leech what money he could from the good-natured peer.

All the time he thus marched on through the hostile French night land, Fox watched his landmarks, guiding his direction by the path and his distance by the subtended angles of the stars. When his guide star was occulted by a black mass that rose stark against the sky, he knew he had arrived.

He halted. The column came to a standstill, and in the silence he could hear sixty men all striving to keep their breathing as soft as possible. He'd have to unleash them soon; they'd burst else.

He looked towards the inlet.

81

Grey knew what to do. *Minion* was shallow-draughted enough to turn in the inlet and even if her bow or stern grounded they could shove her off. He just hoped Grey would be able to get the timing right. That was always the most tricky part of any operation, day or night. Grey had done well that time they'd taken the old *Maria*. That seemed an awfully long time ago. He'd acquired a kind of notoriety over that business, a sniggering laughter behind his back. Men in the Service would talk of Fox's Patent Boarding Brothel with great glee, and that made them overlook the fact that he had taken a Spanish three-decker first rate. She'd burned, afterwards, though . . . What days they had been, swanning around in the Mediterranean!

Alfred Blythe pointed.

Now Fox saw the dark shape gliding up the inlet. Grey was using the sweeps. The wind would serve for the return; but the chance of observation by a sentry was lessened if that sleepy sentry did not have a pile of canvas to occult the stars. Fox saw, indeed, that Grey was well up to time.

He gripped Mr. Smith and nodded towards the gate of the fort.

The gate opened on to the landward side. All the inlet side would be sheer stone, a glacis leading up to the wall and the ramparts with their gun-filled embrasures.

The gunner set off followed by the hands detailed to carry the powder.

Fox went with them, and Blythe remained with the balance. Now was a time to test Mr. Blythe fully. The fight up the Roulet had been interesting; but this was an entirely different kettle of fish. No one spoke. The darkness hung about them and the silence remained. Not even the cry of a night bird broke that stillness. The very silence worried Fox. He could not hear *Min-*

ion; but she must be making noise. And, surely, that damned sentry on the ramparts must see her soon . . .

Fox made sure Mr. Smith dumped the powder kegs neatly by the gate. He did not use them all. There might be other gates inside . . .

Fox waited.

Then, like a bell signalling some bout of fisticuffs on the Downs, the fore six-pounder banged from *Minion.*

Quickly the sounds melded into one rippling roar as *Minion* fired her starboard carronades.

Eight thirty-two pounder carronades, double-shotted and with grape shoved down on top, burst into a staggering uproar after the silence.

Gouts of fire lit the scene. Fox could see the outline of the fort, the flagstaff, the chequered light through the embrasures, and the luridly reflected glare off *Minion* in the background. All hell broke loose.

"Now, Mr. Smith!"

The match took at the first thrust of the tinder, the match fizzed and snaked, the match behaved splendidly. Quick match, fast-burning, cut short—the powder piled at the gate blew up in grand style.

Before the last of the débris had fallen, before the smoke had cleared, with the massive ringing of the eruption still in his ears, George Abercrombie Fox yelled and sprang forward through the shattered gateway.

Tredowan followed. Blythe, the master's mates, Sergeant Dunn and his marines, all were whooping and yelling and roaring in through the gate. This fort was small built to afford protection to Panterre from any cheeky cutting-out expedition the British might chance against the village and the coasters who huddled below. The back door, as usual, was a weak affair. The English went through raving.

Fox saw a sentry staggering about, his hands clasped to his face. He could be ignored. Fox hared on, Etienne bounded at his side, wildly excited, brandishing a pistol and a sabre, yelling "This way!"

They roared after the Frenchman.

Now they were haring past the magazines. Bewildered gunners were staggering out of their barracks beyond, and Dunn had his marines lined up, cool and calm. At Dunn's order the first volley flamed. The gunners pitched face down, riddled, or ran, shrieking. Smoke wafted down. Now the dark lanterns carried could be brought out, carefully! The British raced past the magazines, and Blythe left to do his special work. Fox knew about blowing up magazines. He had a sabre cut in his hat to prove it.

But he must leave that to Blythe now.

On they ran. Now they were up against the centre wall. The Fort was built as any normal fort of the time would be constructed. Star-shaped curtain walls, embrasured for guns, fronted the inlet. At the rear lay an open space, then more walls, with barracks at the side. The magazine had been sited at a lower level and protected by an earthen bank.

Somewhere at the side of the barracks, where the headquarters had been built, that was the target. Etienne said he knew. The stonework looked like new courses on old. *Minion* had scored hits and Fox saw with joy that one of the guns, a thirty-six pounder, had been flung bodily over backwards. Some of the higher masonry, too, had been knocked away.

Minion's damage was not really vital; her distraction of the guard was the vital factor.

She must be pulling up fairly slowly against the set of the current and the wind. The gun's crews must be working like maniacs. Another controlled broadside came in.

Fox yelled: "Duck!"

But Grey knew his shipmates were within the fort. This time he aimed high and used no grape. Still one of the roundshot slammed away a chunk of masonry. Chips flew, No one was hit.

Etienne waved his arms and screamed.

Fox ran across. This was the place.

The men spread out to form a defensive ring. The barracks were alive with noise and lights, now. Soon that company of Boney's infantry would come doubling out.

Fox looked at the door.

A dead French soldier lay outside, his throat slit, and Etienne's sabre showed a dull gleam in the reflected light.

"Open the door, Tredowan," said Fox.

"Aye aye, sir."

The Cornishman put a pistol against the lock and blew it off. Fox kicked the door in. A flash and a bang came from inside. He felt the ball pass his cheek. His own pistol bang-banged and the shadowy figure within screeched and toppled. Fox sprang inside, thrusting the empty pistol at Tredowan.

He drew another and glared about as more men poured through carrying lanterns.

Roland and Jean had been locked in a room which had a barred opening in the door. Roland's face showed, white and blazing in the lantern light.

"Captain Fox!"

"I'm deuced glad to see you!" said Fox. "Now kindly stand back whilst we blow the lock from the door."

Roland's face disappeared. Fox blew the lock off.

Tredowan took the pistol. The door opened and Roland stepped out. The countess Jean followed.

"Now, m'sieu, we run!"

The bedlam continued outside. A party of French soldiers had run out of their barracks, still buckling on their equipment, and had been shot down. More had tried. Now they were shooting from the windows, and Sergeant Dunn had moved his marines into the cover of one of the cross walls. Fox squinted around but in the fitful illumination could see no dead British.

"Pass the word!" he bellowed. "Pull back!"

As he told them, so they moved back. The marines came last, firing by sections, half-volleys that peppered against the windows.

"Belay that, sar'nt! Get your men out of it!"

"Very good, sir."

The marines doubled past, their boots ringing on the stone paving.

Now they were at the cross wall.

Blythe was there.

"All ready, sir."

"When we are at the main gate, Mr. Blythe. Not before. And, as you value your skin, not after."

"Aye aye, sir."

This was the strangeness of command. This giving orders to another man to go and do something diabolically dangerous. To order him to do something that in normal circumstances Fox would do himself without thinking. But he was in command, and now must leave even dangerous tasks to his subordinates.

Everyone collected at the main gate, except for Blythe and his party.

"Sar'nt Dunn! Form up and have a go at anything that tries to follow. And mind out for Mr. Blythe."

"Very good, sir."

86

If the times were still good then Grey would have *Minion* turning by now. He ought to come down a lot faster than he'd gone up. Give him another five minutes.

"Mr. Eckersley. Mr. Gruber! Take the men back to the boats. Make it slippy, now."

"Aye aye, sir!" came two voices, one a choked squeak, the other Gruber's atrociously calm tone.

"Sarn't Dunn! Fall back and cover the landing party! I think the Frogs don't know what's hit 'em yet."

"That they don't, sir. Very good, sir."

Now Fox could throw caution to the winds and go see about Blythe.

He almost knocked the lieutenant over as they collided in the crazy light.

"It's going any second, sir!"

"Come on, then!"

They hared back. And now a musket ball rustled past. The French were gathering their scattered wits. They'd be out of the barracks like rabbits with ferrets after them. A rocket soared and burst, showering specks of fire.

Fox cursed.

Minion was coming down into that.

He swung around. Lights were appearing on the battlements. Among the party with Blythe were Tarpy and Taffy. A positive invitation to break into song. Fox would give a taste of music to the French they wouldn't like.

"Tarpy! Knock those whoresons off the ramparts!"

"Aye *aye*, sir!"

Tarpy hadn't had a decent target all night. He'd looked zealously enough. He'd saved his lovely seven-barrelled gun for something worth while. He called the monster Bertha, and he loved her. Now his heavy features lit up with unholy joy.

"Give us a hoick, Taffy," he grunted.

Between them they got the piece levelled.

Now the lights on the ramparts clustered about the first thirty-six pounder. They were loading up there, ready to smash horrible great holes in *Minion* as she pulled past.

"Go on, Tarpy!" whispered Fox, fiercely.

But Tarpy wouldn't be hurried. He took careful aim. He fussed. Then, as another rocket soared and burst, he fired.

The blast flattened the ears back against the head. The soldiers revealed in the illumination toppled like straw-dummies away from the thirty-six pounder. They screeched. Tarpy crowed. "Ain't that a sight, my oath on't!"

"Good shooting, Tarpy! Now let's get to hell outta here!"

So Fox shooed them past, and ran last himself, and so came out of the gunpowder shattered gateway on to the path. He ran back after his men. He felt somewhat pleased with the night's work.

Then he heard the gunfire at his back, and did not turn. That was Grey coming down. *Minion* was firing all her larboard broadside. The crashes sounded in their familiar way, and Fox counted. Then he counted in another, extra-loud detonation, and knew the French had opened fire.

He ran on.

The magazine blew up.

The noise and the blast dwarfed everything that had gone before.

The force took his hat off his head so that he had to make a clutch to hold on to it. Bits of stone and clods of earth and scraps of old iron whistled past his ears. Someone up ahead was hit and yelled, and that made Fox curse at the senselessness of fate.

Here they were at the boats. They all piled in. Tredowan stowed his collection of pistols beneath the thwart and took the tiller. Fox glared out at the inlet.

Yes, bigod! There was *Minion*. Even as he stared so she let off her larboard broadside again. The flashes made a splendid sight. The men set up a cheer as they pulled out and Fox let them.

They were alongside, hooking on, scrambling up. The boats were whipped out even as *Minion* surged on.

Grey was yelling the men up the shrouds on the instant, to shake out the main tops'l and t'garns'l, he already had the foresails set. Now *Minion* picked up speed. If they kept dead centre of the channel they'd be all right. If they piled up—well, that stinking French prison, or that plot of French land still waited for Fox.

Down the inlet they bore on. The wind caught the canvas, puffing, flukey, not to be trusted; but the beetle-pulling of the sweeps counted here. Onward they bore. The purser came up, touching his hat.

"No one killed, sir. Able seaman Jones One has a stone splinter in his arm. He'll live, sir."

"I'm very glad to hear it, Mr. Swindon."

The carpenter came up, touching his hat.

"Nothing touched, sir, nary a scratch on her."

"I'm very glad to hear it, Mr. Shayne."

He was ravenously hungry, yet far too elated to eat. Out of nothing, a quick impulse, a stupid idea of proving himself, he had done the something that Marianne had pleaded for.

He told himself with some firmness he had not done it because she had asked. No naval officer could allow

89

that sort of interference, maudlin, sentimental and dangerous, to interfere with carrying out his duty.

He'd done it, he supposed, to spite Lord Lymm. That unpleasant character would have crowed in great glee if Fox had trailed in miserably, his tail between his legs, to report failure. There was much to be accomplished tonight before *Minion* could resume her normal ways as a unit of the fleet. On the morrow Fox would take the Blancs out to Lymm's *Meteor*. He would have to ask Roland and the countess Jean what they wished to do and where they desired to be set down. Taking them in and dropping them in France would appear marvellously easy. He'd even let young Grey take them. That would prove something, bigod!

He'd go to Lord Lymm as brazen-faced as a temple-maiden. He'd wear his brand-new full dress commander's uniform. He'd had his old lieutenant's uniforms done over, the white facings removed, the white edging stripped off. A clever sempstress had smartened them for him at a fraction of the cost of a new set of uniforms. Oh, yes, he'd put on a show for Lymm.

When, at last, he had an opportunity to relax in an uncomfortable cot lashed beneath the deckbeams, for his cabin was taken by guests of the female variety, he knew he could allow himself to sleep for only a couple of hours or so. Then he must see about checking over the work Grey was doing. *Minion* must look perfect. He knew, well enough, that Lymm would find fault, and send him on another diabolical errand.

CHAPTER NINE

WHEN Fox rejoined, two more gun vessels of similar build to his *Minion* kept strict formation in the squadron, so he knew something was up.

The Blancs barely spoke. They were middle-aged, grey with fatigue, haunted by what horrors they had seen they could not speak of, shrunken. They went across with Fox, Roland and Jean. Fox's report, there in the great aft cabin of *Meteor*, was brief and matter-of-fact. He knew nothing was to be gained by making anything great or heroic out of what had been done up the Le Sarpenter inlet, against the fort of Panterre.

Lymm didn't even bother to congratulate him on having performed his duty.

Lymm was all over the Blancs.

Dismissed, Fox went up on to the deck and the midshipman on the gangway called for his boat. Roland and Jean came up, too. It was an awkward moment.

"Again I must thank you, Captain Fox."

"I think your thanks should extend to my first lieutenant, Mr. Grey. Had he not behaved with extraordinary gallantry, we would not have gone for you that night, and—"

"And those pigs of Bonapartistes would have sent us to Paris, in the morning, in chains!" The countess Jean still wore her man's rig; but nothing could disguise her femininity.

Fox cocked an eye at Roland.

"I still have Etienne and Marianne aboard. I had the thought that Marianne, at least, would accompany you."

"No, Captain Fox. I had never met Marianne until this business—"

"But!"

Roland spread his hands. "I cannot explain the way a woman's mind works." He half turned, with a slight smile, to Jean. "Nor, I fancy, can you, my dear countess."

She made a face, her thin lips stretching. "If you want my opinion I suggest that if women wore men's clothes more frequently they might carry more weight in the affairs of men. But—" and here she laughed, tossing her head back. "But I do not think men would think more clearly if they wore women's clothes!"

"God forbid!" said Fox. The idea of going into action with skirts trailing to the ground appalled him. But women did. He felt for women, then, did G. A. Fox.

He did not offer to shake hands. As he turned to go over the side Jean half-stepped forward, and then halted. Roland said: "Please convey my utmost thanks and congratulations to Mr. Grey, Captain fox."

"It will give me pleasure, sir."

It would, true enough, but—how so to convey those sentiments to the ineffable Mr. Grey without incurring that elegant young man's impious scorn and amused toleration? Fox mused on that, for a space, as he was pulled back to his command, and then his mind turned to the preparations being made in Lord Lymm's small squadron.

Lymm had said nothing. He had given no orders

that might reveal what was afoot. Those two new gun vessels, gunbrigs like *Minion*, signified the squadron was in for action. These little vessels with their shallow draught were armed with an almighty big punch. They could carry a powerful battery into shoal waters where frigates could not go. Some large and formidable enemy was lurking in a cove or a roadstead somewhere along the French coast, and my Lords of the Admiralty had selected Lord Lymm's squadron to go in after them. That could be the only explanation.

Fox wondered just how much the admirals knew of Lord Lymm's character. They'd know that Lieutenant Tobias Curwen was a man on whom his captain could rely. But, beyond that? Fox began to have doubts. Lymm must have played the whole game through without putting a foot wrong.

The action in which *Minion* had just been engaged had been entirely unofficial. Lymm's report would merely say that the spies had been landed and the Blancs brought off. No mention of the destruction of the fort of Panterre would be made. Lymm had not the guts in him to do the job, and he didn't have the guts to brazen through any claim he might make subsequently. All he would see would be glory for Commander Fox. Fox could do without that kind of glory. Glory was for the storybook heroes of schoolboys. So long as he had food, and drink, and a warm dry bed, and could take care of his family—and a compliant woman—generally more interesting than a complaisant woman—then all the glory could go hang.

In the event he merely repeated Roland's words to Grey.

To Fox's intense surprise, Lionel Grey flushed.

"Thank you, sir," said Grey. Then: "It was an

honour, sir, to be of some assistance to you and Mr. Roland."

So that left Fox right in it—up to the neck.

He fixed his arctic-floes of eyes on Grey.

"I should reprimand you most severely for bringing my vessel up that damned inlet, Mr. Grey. Good God! You were sailing right up the arse of Boney's stronghold! You were imperilling the vessel!"

"Aye aye, sir. But, with due respect sir, if you don't mind my saying so, sir, we had plenty of steerage room, the soundings were ample, we-"

Fox glared.

Grey shut up.

So, again, he had to say it.

"I'm much obliged to you, Mr. Grey, for your courageous action. I wouldn't have liked Mr. Roland—or his friend—to have been shot by the Frogs. You did well, sir, confound you for a scheming imp of Satan!"

"Aye aye, sir," said Grey. And so Fox knew he had lost another round with this infernally elegant and supercilious young man.

Now, if John Carker had done all that—as he could, he could!—the good Carker would have regarded it all as merely the obvious thing to have done in the circumstances.

With his usual intolerant eye for perfection Fox had been keeping the mental check upon *Minion* and all who sailed in her. He would solve the problem of the ship's corporal. Grey, of course—and despite his obnoxious affection for Fox—was utterly dependable. Blythe was promising. The two middies were a contrast, and yet—how short a time ago, it seemed, when Mr. Gruber had been just such a squeaking mouse as Eckersley, when he'd had his mouth mangled—and yet they were both promising. The master's mates were competent, knowing their jobs and doing them without fuss. Mr. Watson, the master, was the master fusser. But he was a valuable man. Of the standing officers, Fox could pick not one he would say was useless, and MacMillan, the boatswain, looked more than promising. The marines were, as usual, excellent. The purser— well, old fourteen ounces must learn to knuckle down to the work of the brig, or else. As for the rest, they were the usual mish-mash. Most of them were prest men, a good few had been pressed, and the mixture favoured Fox. He often said he didn't care if a man volunteered or was pressed; once he was under the discipline of the Royal Navy he would turn into a prime seaman or he'd be dead.

Only when on the following day his orders came from Lord Lymm did Fox see the fuller significance of this running tally of the efficiency of his command he kept always in his head. Once Lieutenant Ashley Haines had left—and the quicker that vicious puppy left his vessel the better Fox liked it—Fox looked at the orders and was staggered.

There was to be an operation; but Lymm did not even put the name of the place or the force to be found there in the orders. He could excuse that on the grounds of secrecy. There was to be an attack. Lymm's *Meteor*, clearly, would act as flagship, and Fox surmised that the noble lord would keep her well offshore as the gun vessels went in. *Prosperity*, the sloop, would act as liaison. The four gun vessels, *Darter* with the shallowest draught inshore of the others, would make the attack. Commander Dodson in *Glowworm* would command the inshore force. Well, Dodson had three months seniority over Fox. There was no fault to be found there. The other two gun vessels, Commander Green's *Spanker* and Commander Cotton's *Selby*, newly joined, would form a considerable force with power sufficient in their massed broadsides of thirty-two pounder carronades to have a devastating effect on the frigates that, surmised Fox, would be their targets and victims.

He could only surmise.

The orders contained no instructions as to where *Minion* would figure in the scheme. And then came the part that shook Fox to his keelson.

Over two thirds of his ship's company were to be transferred—forthwith—to the other vessels of the inshore force so as to bring them fully up to complement.

Fox gaped.

He just sat there, like a loon, his jaw hanging open.

Lord Lymm—Captain Lord Lymm—was stripping *Minion* so as to cram as many men as possible into the vessels taking part in the attack. The orders brought a shattering sense of defeat to Fox.

The bastard!

Fox saw it all, in a twinkling, saw it clear and horrible and deadly.

Lymm knew what he was doing. The enemy force must be sufficient for their Lordships at the Admiralty to consider it wise to take them, or destroy them. Lymm knew the forces to be engaged. He must have calculated, with Mr. Curwen to assist him, that the four gun vessels could do it. Therefore it would be a sound scheme to cram them with me. Fox knew the real reason was simply so that Lymm might baulk him from taking part in the action, from gaining some recognition, achieving some renown, and thus making another stride forward to shifting his swab.

Posting receded once more on to the distant horizon.

Fox dare not say anything aloud. He had to sit there and digest this news. There was another sheet of paper with the orders, and this he took and began to read in a mechanical way, hardly conscious of what it said. Then understanding penetrated and a second thrilling shock scorched through him.

This was a list of personnel to be shipped across to the other vessels.

He read as though bereft of his senses.

Lymm detailed the names and ranks of those men he wanted. There was Blythe, and Kilmartin and Longbridge, most of the foretopmen, there was Eckersley, a whole crowd of quarter gunners and gun captains, a gaggle of idlers. Fox felt bewilderment. At first he could see no rhyme or reason to it. Surely, having once been ordered to furnish a certain number of men, it should be left to himself, surely, to detail the men to go?

And then the pattern emerged.

Oh, these men were not the old Raccoons.

But he saw that the men to remain with him were men in whom he felt confidence, hands who showed a stronger feeling of loyalty to the captain than the others. The demarcation lines were of necessity hazy. Many good men were detailed to go. But, on balance, and supposing Fox were to detail a crew to go with him on some desperate enterprise, the men he would have chosen were the men excluded from Lymm's list.

That meant only one thing.

One of his own officers must be passing information to Lymm. Someone, here in this vessel, must be telling that whoreson Lord Lymm just who was kindly disposed towards Commander Fox. So that Lymm could be absolutely safe and take those men who didn't give a fig for Fox.

Fox looked at his mahogany-hard hands, square and powerful, lying spread on the papers before him. Those hands began to curl together, rounding, constricting. It was most curious. He couldn't stop the action. He knew that if Lymm's neck were between those constricting fists he'd go on squeezing.

A knock sounded and Grey came in.

Fox looked up. God knew what his eyes looked like, what the expression on his face; but Grey said, sharply: "Is anything the matter, sir?"

"No," he managed to say. His hands relaxed. "No, Mr. Grey. We have our orders from Captain Lord Lymm."

Grey fired up.

"That is indeed good news, sir."

"It is the most goddammed bad news, Mr. Grey!"

"Sir?"

Fox threw the orders and the list across the desk at Grey. Grey caught them, smoothed them out, turned them up the right way and read. Presently he looked up at Fox. The expression on Grey's face was unreadable.

"I—see, sir."

Fox was not yet himself.

"I'm sure you do, Mr. Grey. This comes of wenching and drinking in Tunbridge Wells. You would have done better to have found yourself a captain who could—who could—"

"Sir!" Grey took the enormous risk of cutting in. "Sir! Commander Fox! I—" Then Grey, too, realised he could not put into bald words all the turmoil of his emotions.

So they faced each other, Mr. Grey and Commander Fox. They thought a great deal, their emotions were real and tearing; but they could say nothing to each other.

"Very good, Mr. Grey." Fox bashed it out, now, the hurt conquered, the wound staunched, the blood

98

drying. "Rouse out the hands to go. See they look presentable. And make damn sure we remain on station in the squadron."

"Aye aye, sir."

Grey left.

Well—what the hell was there to say, anyway?

Though the vessel trilled the bosun's calls, the stamp and rush of naked horny feet over the planking, the yells as men were sorted out. Dunnage would be taken, they must be issued with weapons and take their hammocks, too—just the one each would be sufficient. The orders were explicit. Lieutenant Curwen had written them, that was clear. Fox began to wonder if he would have to deal with Curwen, too. Curwen was a crusty old sea-dog, doing a job. Probably he hated and despised Lymm as much as Fox. He didn't have the same reasons, though, that was for sure.

When the men had gone Commander Fox went up onto the deck of *Minion*. He walked right aft, past the tiller, and stood against the taffrail, looking out to the horizon. The weather remained clear and there was heat still in the sun and the waves ran with that longer rhythm that told of earlier disturbances far out into the Atlantic. The Channel was a real hodge-podge of a sea to sail. Anything could happen and invariably did. Fox stood there for some time, hearing the sounds of his command muted and distant, a half-dream from a world from which he could never be parted without a sense of loss and yet a world which despised him and which he detested if it did not conform to his will.

How much power had a lowly commander? Massive power within the wooden walls of his ship. Practically none outside, where he would come up against captains and admirals engaged in the perennial struggle for power, one against another, clique against clique. He'd almost be better off back as first lieutenant to Captain Percy Staunton. But that would be to throw back the interest Staunton had shown in him. Admiral Cloughton, too, must have had a hand in getting Fox promoted into *Minion*. He began at this time to consider if a letter to Staunton and Cloughton might be risked. He had no way of knowing for sure how they judged him, what they felt about him as a person, whether both had fixed *Minion* for him as a reward for services rendered. Having done that, they might both consider the account closed. Fox would understand that.

He might make matters worse. He didn't even know how Lord Lymm stood with Cloughton. Had it been Captain Stone, now, Toady Stone, he would know exactly what Cloughton thought.

He roused himself. The sun was sinking. With only himself, Grey and Partridge, it was clear he would have to stand a watch himself. He must go through the watch-bill with Grey and draw up a fresh listing of the men and their duties. He had been left with such a skeleton crew that a nincompoop like Lymm would believe he could only either sail or fight, but not do both.

He heard someone coming up behind him, and then Grey's tickle of a tactical cough, and he turned, his face its usual stony gargoyle.

"Yes, Mr. Grey?"

"It's Etienne and Marianne, sir. What are we to do with them?"

He hadn't forgotten them. Other things had been more pressing, and here 'things' meant unmentionable disasters and grievances.

"Have we been left with enough hands to man a boat, Mr. Grey?" Fox spoke with a heavy humourless sarcasm.

"They express a desire to be set ashore, sir. But not up Le Sarpenter. It's likely to be a trifle too hot right now."

"I'm sure it is."

Midshipman Gruber yelled. He was squinting over towards *Meteor.*

"Flagship's signalling, sir!" Then at the string of black balls that rose into the air, Gruber clutched his telescope and prepared to read off the flags. The new signal book could only bring Fox more grief, he supposed, most dully.

When the signal was deciphered it gave Fox orders to take the prizes under his lee and to wait for the return of the flagship.

"What damned prizes?" snarled Fox, glaring about the darkening horizon.

"We're ordered to wait the return of *Meteor,*" pointed out Grey, "and she ain't left yet. Maybe he's talking about the prizes he *intends* to bring out."

"Devil take the man!" said Fox, rather incautiously, seeing that Gruber was within earshot.

But Gruber was most anxious to prove himself, now that he had been left aboard in a position of lonely authority among his absent peers—Partridge was a good fellow and loyal, but lacking in the finer spirit, or so conceived young Mr. Midshipman Gruber. Now he shinnied halfway up the shrouds, and shaded his eyes to peer into the orange and gold glory of the sunset and the glitter from the sea.

"There's *Prosperity,* sir!" he cried. "An' she's got four sail with her. Coasters, sir—"

Prosperity must have taken these four fine fat fish when she'd been scouting. Prosperity by name and prosperous by nature. Well, Commander Stamp-Clayton would be highly popular with Lymm. Those four coasters were deeply-laden and worth a packet, if they were lucky as to cargoes. One thing that Lymm would not fail to point out was that they weren't laden down with the kind of merchandise Commander Fox liked to take—sea-water.

"Make a signal to the flagship," said Fox. "Acknowledge. Signal to *Prosperity's* prizes. Take station under my lee."

"Aye aye, sir," shrilled Gruber and he hurled himself off the shrouds and at the signal lockers.

For Mr. Midshipman Gruber, who remembered this madman Fox in the confusing and frightening turmoil of the action of *Furieuse* with *Zodiaque*, the doings at the fort of Panterre had smacked of heroism. Gruber had had his mouth mangled when old Furry-arse clawed at the big *Zodiaque*. He could remember Fox's concern. And in the enormous battle that was now called Cloughton's Action, young Gruber had seen Mr. Fox acting the very admiral, to the life. To Gruber, then, it seemed passing strange that Commander Fox always got the dirty end of the stick. Captain Staunton, who had been kindness itself to Gruber's family—he fancied his sister Dolly had something to do with that, poor though the family was—had simply told Gruber that if he wished to continue at sea he might with the greatest confidence sail with Commander Fox. Mr. Midshipman Felix Gruber had agreed.

So now, as he saw that the correct flags went up the halliards in the correct sequence, young Gruber wondered about the destiny of great men, and if he would ever wear the epaulettes of a captain, and one day hoist his own flag.

The prizes detached themselves from the protection of *Prosperity* and soon, and somewhat clumsily, manoeuvred themselves under *Minion's* lee. Fox guessed they were damnably short-handed, their prize-crews as stingy as possible and had barely enough men to handle the craft.

Night recognition signals would remain in force. When the sun at last sank Fox sailed in company with ten other vessels. When the sun rose again he would be left with merely the four prizes to guard. A scatter of uninhabited islands within the wider sweep of the bay, called the Remplades, was to be the selected site of his waiting. There, so Lord Lymm giving his orders with the grim form of Mr. Curwen at his elbow, Fox would find shelter and some secrecy from discovery by hostile shipping until the squadron returned.

Very well, then! He'd sit it out. He'd damn well take care of these prizes, keeping the potential prize money intact for Lymm. He damn well would do his duty and obey orders. And then, afterwards, he'd see about stirring up a hornet's nest and throwing this oaf Lymm off his back.

With that settled it was in a much more resolved frame of mind he stood his watch. Even this experience came afresh to him, with the smack of an old joy rediscovered. Standing a watch could be the most tiresome bore in the world. It could also be a time for self-discovery, of self-analysis. It was a time to run through what one knew of life, of fascinating investigations into the ways of the sea, and of surmounting all manner of hideous possibilities that could only occur in nightmares—or as routine on the blockade of Brest, for instance.

He came off watch in a most peculiar frame of mind.

Lymm was going to be cut down to size, that was certain.

He barged into his cabin, threw off his hat and

loosened his neckcloth and a woman's voice said: "Is that you, Etienne?"

Fox stopped in mid-action, his hand gripping his neck cloth, his face expressive of the utmost consternation. Then he moved like a horse kicked in the rump, found flint and steel, struck and caught the tinder, blew the flame into life and so lit the lantern.

Marianne sat up in her cot, her hair falling about her face, her eyes sleepy, her cheeks flushed. Her white shirt hung ruffled and open down her bosom, revealing the twin symmetrical curves. She stretched, lazily, blinking.

"Oh! It is you, George. You startled me."

The marine sentry at the door!

Then reason re-asserted itself. Everyone knew the French lady dressed up as a man had been quartered in the commander's cabin.

"Your pardon, madame," began Fox.

"Come now, George! None of your flummery! I saw you in the safe house. I know what you're after."

Bigod!

Well, it was true enough, the Good Lord Harry knew.

"I misjudged the time," said Fox. He couldn't say he had forgotten she was here, for he possessed a memory of formidable strength, didn't he? Well, then, what with the exertions of the past hours, with Lymm's atrocious treatment of him, with the exercises to keep up his morale during his time on watch—well, of course he'd known she was here. He just hadn't been thinking about it. Sheer habit had brought him down and into his own cabin.

"I will retire at once, Marianne."

She slid a long and shockingly naked leg from the cot.

"Corbleu! You will do no such thing!"

He stared at her. He knew what was going to happen to his left eyeball—and, yes, here it came. That pink and black ring came dropping softly down over his left eye, without pain or irritation, like some erotic benediction for passion.

She sat on the edge of the cot, and her legs gleamed in the lanternlight. Those legs were exceedingly lovely in the sight of a lecherous old sailorman.

"You stare so, George! If I did not know what you are thinking, I would get the shudders!"

Fox did not laugh. But he did manage a throaty kind of chuckling growl.

"If you know, then you should shudder."

"I can see through you—" Her shirt was slipping dangerously over her left shoulder. He could see the skin of her shoulder, rounded and smooth with the shape of the bone beneath, gleaming in the lanternlight. He put his neckcloth down, somewhere. She smiled again. She reached out her arm to him, her fingers crooked, beckoning.

"George! Come here—"

They were speaking French. But that marine sentry out there would recognise and understand the tone of voice; he was a man and he would know what the husky endearments would mean, the soft entreating breath, French or English.

Fox crossed to her and put a finger on her mouth.

She tried to bite him, laughing.

"Marianne! There is a sentry—"

"I know! I do believe, George, you have the power of the devil over these stiff-backed men of yours. He treated me as though I was a child, or an old lady—or truly a man."

"Bigod, he'd better have!" said Fox, outraged.

"But—"

"Now no buts. If you don't care for your reputation—"

She laughed again; but this time the laugh was much softer and lower and all the more exciting for that. "If you think a woman may wear a man's clothes and retain any reputation whatsoever, then you dream—"

"I've known a few girls to wear men's clothes, and fine gals they were, too! That's not what I mean. I'm the captain. I can't fornicate with a gal in my cabin and let all the hands know!"

A wayward thought crossed Fox's mind. When that black swine Lord Lymm had stripped his command of men he hadn't taken the marines, probably because there was no landing contemplated. He'd left Sergeant Dunn and his men. Now, with marine Cowley standing ram-rod stiff outside his door, Fox could have wished Lymm to have taken 'em all.

"I shall not make a sound," said Marianne. Clearly, or so it seemed to G. A. Fox, she was aroused, passionate, and if he wasn't the man to let slip an opportunity like this, he equally wasn't the man to ruin ship's discipline. That no-good bully Harvey, the ship's corporal, had—and very surprisingly—been on the list of those selected by Lymm. The hands must have nothing to suspect. If they knew their captain was tumbling a French girl in the cabin—

"George! Why do you not pay me attention?"

Fox reached out and managed to find his neckcloth. He began to fumble it around his neck.

"I'll come back in ten minutes. Don't go away."

She panted at him. She flicked the tip of her pink tongue out over her lips. Her hair shone with more corngold in it than brown. Her incipient moustache could not distract Fox now. He found his hat. "Wait for me."

He barged out of his door and was in time to catch marine Cowley not quite at attention.

Fox ignored that. He had a scheme to work.

"Keep a sharp lookout, Cowley. The Frenchlady's been having bad dreams. I'll be back directly. So keep alert!"

"Very good, sir," shouted marine Cowley.

If he was surprised at the order, possibly imagining that Fox would send him away, Fox could feel gratification that he could think three jumps ahead of a cloth-headed marine.

He barged along making a great deal of noise, clattering up on to the quarterdeck. Everything proceeded smoothly. *Minion* kept to her station, dog-legging about, beating up and then running free—not too often, for Fox didn't want his men up all night—but sufficiently to be an annoyance.

Fox prowled about the quarterdeck for perhaps five minutes. *Minion* was due to make one of her changes of course in the next few moments, and it was clear that the captain had come on deck to see just how well it would be managed. That, considered Fox, served admirably.

He thought of Marianne, sitting there on his cot, naked but for her man's shirt, with her long legs and the shadows, and the way her hair fell about her face, and that gleam from her shoulder, and he knew he was hot, damned hot.

Just as Grey, who had the deck, was about to yell, Fox clumped below again. That should make 'em buzz.

To marine Cowley he said: "All clear?"

"All clear, sir."

He might have ordered Cowley aloft to help. Lord knew, even a marine would be useful so short-handed were they. But the imp of mischief in Fox was having full sway. If he was going to tumble Marianne with a marine standing guard at the door then wouldn't that add a little piquancy to it all? A little spice to the occasion?

He shut the door behind him; but not before he said, in English, for Cowley's benefit: "I trust you are feeling better madame. I shall prescribe a few drops my doctor recommends, and I thoroughly endorse his prescription."

Let Cowley work that one out.

Marianne stared at him with her blue eyes round. She really did look lovely, and he could always slip his eyes, as it were, over the moustache and dwell on more fascinating aspects of her face and figure.

He put a hand to his lips.

"You are ravishing, Marianne,"—and he meant it.

She smiled and, again, held out her hands to him.

This time George Abercrombie Fox was across the cabin and grasping her like a rattlesnake. Above their heads the deck resounded and sang to the sounds of men working the brig. Well, poor devils, they weren't the captain. The captain was down here, in his cabin, with his hands full of hot feminine flesh, and a delightful girl was struggling to remove his neckcloth and his shirt, and occasionally biting his ear and then giving him a nip on the shoulder. Fox nipped her back. She squealed. So he had to kiss her.

The kiss lasted.

During that kiss they made themselves fairly comfortable, and there were two men's shirts on the deck below the cot, and the cot was swinging—gently, gently—for Fox knew the ways of giving a woman pleasure. She understood that he knew, too, and she demanded everything he knew and would give. Even so, even so—damnably so—every confounded time he thought of Sophy. He thought of Sophy at least six times that night.

CHAPTER TEN

THE morning dawned depressingly damp and grey, with a drifting drizzle. Fox felt physically extraordinarily lively. He'd stood his watch. Marianne was asleep now, and marine Bodger stood guard on the door. Etienne was up and about, making unfavorable comments about the weather. Mr. Grey was about and Minion rumbled to all the normal sounds of men preparing for the day, holystoning the deck—a useless task but one conducive to discipline and to appeasing first lieutenants' tempers—and soon the hammocks would come up, and burgoo and all the old familiar routine would roll on from bell to bell.

The four prizes followed Minion. The bay was barely visible to the south, and Fox frowned. They must edge a little into the offing. He wanted no observation of him from shore.

He could judge the course and knew that the shoreline would drop away in five minutes. Being G. A. Fox. he decided to let the five minutes elapse with his command functioning as normal, rather than create further trouble. A gentle movement of the tiller and Minion edged away. At four and three quarter minutes precisely the land dropped below the horizon.

Away to the north lay the scatter of uninhabited islands known as the Remplades. One could play ducks and drakes there in fine style. There were shoals and reefs, of course. One could rip a ship's bottom there as easily as anywhere. Fox's orders whilst he waited called on him to use the Remplades as cover. Well, that might prove interesting. There was that confounded fog to consider, also.

Lymm had not had the effrontery to take the standing officers from the brig. Fox would have queried that order at once, taking the risk in the—fairly—secure assumption that he might have Captain Lord Lymm by the short and curlies. But enough of speculation, for he had to discuss the gunner's accounts now.

"We fired away a mighty lot, sir," said Mr. Smith in the tones of any long-service warrant officer talking about actually using the supplies for which he was responsible. "An' there's them half-barrels we blew the gate in with—"

"Yes, yes," cried Fox. "We had a lovely bang, as you my recall. Now how do we stand as regards the half-barrels we have left?"

Mr. Smith had employed the white large-grain powder to blow the gate down, with a single keg of the red large-grain which he had fused and so blown up first. That had made sure of the explosion. White grain powder, the reconstituted stuff, was nowhere near as reliable as fresh, nor as powerful, neither, sir, as Mr. Smith would say.

Sometimes, as now, Fox could wish for Joachim, that gunner's mate of extraordinary competence. But Mr. Smith was efficient and willing, and: "That was good thinking on your part, Mr. Smith."

"Thank 'ee, sir." Then Mr. Smith ventured. "I'm mortal glad you wuz able to secure the extra powder over our allocation, sir. We'm using the stuff mortal fast."

111

"And I hope we shall use it some more, Mr. Smith."

Fox knew of captains who were frightened to exercise their guns for fear of the want of powder when real action came. Fox was a poor man. All the money he could spare must go to his mother, his sisters and brothers, aged aunts and all his relations in the old row house by the Thames. He had made some money gambling at cards, and a little of the accrued prize money had trickled through from Snellgrove and Dupre; not much, he had not so far been a lucky officer where prize money was concerned. All the same, poor though he was, he had known where money would buy kegs of powder. Good new large-grain red, too. The country must be in a sad state of corruption where serving officers had to bribe and corrupt dockyard officials to obtain essential supplies for their commands, but he was used to it. Changes were coming, and ward-room gossip had been that old Jarvie, Lord Saint Vincent, was really going to do something. Fox awaited the day.

Having settled Mr. Smith's accounts, Fox went through Mr. Swindon's. Here was such a maze of figures, such a marvellous discursiveness, such a twisting, that many and many a captain had thrown his hands up in despair. After all, pursers had to pay so much money as a bond to secure their employment and the poor devils had to get it back somehow, hadn't they? Fox was quite prepared to go down every column of figures, to follow every entry to the bitter end, to trace the consumption of every last item. Purser's dips, no less than slops, no less than the very barrels of salt pork, the split peas, no less than every single item—G. A. F. wouldn't let any damned purser hoodwink him and thus bring discontent to his crew.

The carpenter made his report, and Fox nodded, satisfied. His first lieutenant would already have checked

112

everything before this. At least, Fox assumed Grey would have done so. It was an elementary precaution to take.

He felt remarkably at ease, standing on his own quarter-deck, happily immersed in the fascinating details of shipboard life, able to talk technicalities with his warrant officers. Maybe the small boy who had been a wide-eyed powder monkey in the old *Henrietta*, and who had seen the grave and serious warrant officers talking arcane lore, peeked out of Fox during these moments.

Yes, given that what he was doing was worthwhile—as it was, it was!—he felt reasonably content. He had thought that he only needed to keep his nose clean and he was sure to be posted, having reached commander's rank. He had been baulked of going on this expedition; but there would be others. He'd settle Lymm's hash for him. After that, he would stand a chance. The anger might flow at thought of the time he was wasting; but he was past worrying about that. Next birthday, next month, he'd be thirty five. An old man in the race for an admiral's stakes. To be an admiral at an age when you were not yet senile you needed to be posted as early as you could, certainly by the age of twenty-one.

Just keeping his nose clean was certainly proving difficult with Lymm around. But even that thought could not disturb his eerie equanimity. The wind blew fresher, *Minion* stood on grandly, the men were kept busy—and down below in his cabin lay sleeping a girl who had—and, bigod!—who would again before he let her off his command!

She would be leaving tonight. Grey would take her and Etienne ashore. Very well, then. He had the day in which to make a beast of himself.

113

About the fourth or fifth bout, Fox rose for air to hear the yelling from the upper deck—the only deck, as *Minion* was all a mess of platforms below—and heard the horny patter of feet. The bosun's calls shrilled. Soon, as sure as fate, a messenger would come banging into his cabin. He rolled off, with a groan, and heard the marine sentry saying something just loud enough for him to hear the sound without catching the words.

"Belay there!" bellowed Fox. He hauled up his old trousers and shrugged on his coat, feeling the epaulette weighing down all one-sidedly. He made himself presentable in double-quick time. Marianne disappeared beneath the blankets on the cot. Fox flumped himself down at his desk and snatched up a quill.

"Come in!" he bellowed.

The ship's boy—it was little Peter Pettigrew, all pimples and dimples and a mass of fair curly hair—stuttered: "Please sir, fust lootenan's complimens, sir, an' will you step up on't deck, sir, please, sir!"

You just couldn't get rough and tough with little urchins like this. Fox could recall with nostalgic horror his own first carryings of messages about the gloomy and cavernous mysteries of *Henrietta*.

"Thank you, Pettigrew. My compliments to the first lieutenant and I will step up on deck."

"Aye aye, sir!"

Peter Pettigrew scampered away. He had knuckled his forehead twice. He had carried a message to the august presence of the captain. Gruber, as a midshipman, was now a cut above that kind of work, being the only midshipman in the brig. Pettigrew was a bright lad. He would be worth fostering. Fox wondered how Ben Ferris was faring. Then he stomped out on deck and saw what all the fuss was about.

The whole western horizon showed a band of angry copper. The wind had faded. The sea ran greasily.

"You won't be setting the French people ashore tonight, Mr. Grey," said George Abercrombie Fox.

"No, sir. And we won't be dropping the hook in the Remplades, either, sir, the Devil take it!"

The flurry of activity continued as *Minion* snugged down for the coming blow. Channel gales were nasty beasts. They were unpredictable to the extent that they might do any number of unconscionably horrid things, unlike those gales in other parts of the world where the weather obeyed some kind of overall laws. The filthy stuff was coming in from the west, and that was about the only item of regularity about what followed. *Minion* was flung fiercely about. She proved herself to be the terror of a sea-boat she was: wet, cranky, a cow to manage, giving all the souls in her moments of heart-stopping terror. But she survived. By the time the gale at last blew itself out, rumbling and grumbling, and Fox could set a course that would bring them up with the Remplades just after first light, he could look about and feel thankful they had survived.

The four prizes likewise survived. They crept along to the rendezvous, bedraggled, battered; but still afloat. Fox once more fumed at the stupidity of Lymm's orders. Just because he wanted to see the prizes in himself he had kept them here. Any sane commander— there were a few to be found somewhere in the Royal Navy, a few—would have sent the prizes in at least to Saint Paul's Harbour, if not to Saint Helier, even with the scarecrow prize-crews aboard.

The devil of it was that Captain Lord Lymm would have a perfect set of reasons for his actions. When they were trotted out, Fox knew with a sour despair that no one would think to question them—for the prizes were

115

there, were they not, riding under the guns of Lord Lymm's little squadron? How the man had managed to be given a whole squadron to command, even if it was only a motley collection of gun vessels, escaped Fox. The bastard's seniority was low, still, and even our Percy was senior.

Marianne crept out on to the deck. She wore a massive old boat-cloak that Tredown had found for her. She looked palely green and fragile; but she could find a smile for him. Fox touched his hat.

"Good morning, madame."

In her rapid and slurred French that Fox knew came from an affectation of Paris speech patterns, she said: "You left me all night so suffer, George! I might have died! It was horrible!"

"Yet you are here, alive and well, and exceedingly lovely." The early sun cast a betraying shadow over her upper lip, and Fox looked away, over the western heave of the sea. Landsdowne, who might be a second Wilson one day, perched in the main crosstrees. If he had not spotted the Remplades yet, they were not in sight.

"George!"

"Please, madame! I will step below in a few moments. But the vessel must be worked. There is much to do."

Marianne could see that, anyway. The hands were busy about the deck, clearing up after the night's chaos.

"Very well. But do not keep me waiting long."

She would wait until the islands were descried, that was for sure.

Grey and Watson were deep in conversation on the lee side of the quarterdeck. Fox overheard Watson fussing about some miniscule detail, and Grey's light laugh, and his: "Deuce take it, Mr. Watson! I would dearly like to know how Captain Lymm has fared over last night."

Fox would like to know that, too.

There would have been precious little fighting done last night in the gale. Would Lymm hang about in the offing and make a fresh attempt this day, or night, or would he return to the Remplades, to find out how his precious prizes had survived? Fox knew what he would do. He supposed Curwen, to give Lymm's first lieutenant his due, would do the same.

He took a turn around the cramped little quarterdeck.

Lord knew what mischief this gale had let loose. Every time a gale broomed up the Channel and the British either had to run for cover or face crippling losses, the blockade of France—and notably hereabouts the unceasing blockade of Brest—came adrift. It happened infrequently enough, to be sure, and Fox felt pretty confident that last night's gale would have not disturbed the massive power of the ships of the line if his flat-bottomed old tub of a *Minion* had survived. Trouble was, the two-deckers couldn't afford to run too far to leeward, for something might slip out from a French port. This was the time when the privateers made their dashes to clear the British patrols and make for the outer seas. There was always a steady trickle of French privateers slipping out, of course, and a fine kettle of fish they made among the convoys; but gales tended to wedge open the gates wider than any admiral could view with comfort.

When the Remplades were at last sighted, and Landsdowne bellowed the information to the deck, Fox remained where he was. Marianne was undeniably delightful; the sweet firmness of her, the length of her legs, the roundness of her thighs, the way she kissed—

117

charming, charming, and something a lecherous old sailorman like George Abercrombie Fox would cherish; but, here he was, searching a hostile sea and jagged rocks for hostile ships. Just one smart corvette would play havoc with the prizes. A chasse maree would do the business just as well. This was no time to step below, madame, no matter what sinful glories awaited him there.

The morning remained fresh. There was no fog this morning, the gale had swept that away. The sea remained lumpy from the violence of the night. The wind, still brisk although tending to a dying fall which indicated that it might turn flukey as the sun climbed, blew from the west south west. All these conditions were perfectly ordinary. *Minion* sailed under all plain sail on the starboard tack, running in to the land, invisible over the southern horizon. In a few moments she would have to tack and so run back out to the Remplades on the larboard tack. The wind was almost dead foul for a direct approach.

Fox was not happy with the handling of his brig in this breeze and with the amount of canvas he had hung out. Now that he'd actually sighted the islands he could give orders to hand the main and fore topgallant sails. She'd ride easier now and the prizes could come up in their own time. His dissatisfaction, which persisted in every ship in which he sailed no matter that he loved them all, could now sensibly diminish.

Landsdowne had yelled down no sighting, so Lymm had presumably not turned back but had decided to stick it out for another day's effort.

Minion tacked. The evolution was carried out smartly enough by the hands, and with Grey giving the orders Fox knew the job would be done properly. Even so the gunbrig made heavy weather of it, and for a fraction of a second Fox thought Grey had lost her. Then the rudder bit and the canvas shimmied and stiffened and they were laying over on the larboard tack and *Minion* had once again proved herself a viable sailing vessel—but only just.

When Grey resumed his watchful place on the quarterdeck he naturally shifted over to the lee side. Fox felt no need to make any comments about the evolution. One tack more or less ought to make little difference in a sea officer's life; very soon Fox was to discover just how great a difference that tack had made. Had Grey botched it, had they carried away a spar, had they hung up, had anything untoward happened, then Landsdowne would not have sung out: "Sail ho!" at just the time he did, nor would *Minion* have been in the place she was, and the prizes would not—would most certainly not—have been crewed by British jack tars.

Before Grey could bellow back: "Where away?" Landsdowne had shouted again. "Deck there! Fine on the larboard bow! Looks like a lugger, sir—"

"Lay me horizontal!" burst out Mr. Grey. "A confounded French privateer lugger! After our prizes, too, may the devil take him."

"Hardly our prizes, Mr. Grey," said Fox with a curious calmness that made Grey jerk around, flushed of face. "But as to the rest of your sentiments, I am entirely in accord."

Fox lifted his voice in that coarse lower-deck bellow that could flay a man's ear in the foretop in a gale.

"Any more sail in sight?"

The tiny interval before Landsdowne answered pleased Fox. The man had looked again, a quick sweeping survey, just to confirm no other sail danced at the limit of observation.

"Nary a one, sir!"

"Then I think we may look forward to a brisk action and a prize of our own," said Commander George Abercrombie Fox with a bright and breezy briskness that jolted everyone in hearing. "That is," he added with the effect of a cold douche, "if the bastard stays to fight."

He looked over at the four prizes sloshing along. They looked a miserable bunch; but there was no disguising what they were—richly-laden coasters packed with goodies originally destined for Bonaparte's France and now diverted to the avaricious fingers of John Bull. Surely no Frenchman worth his salt would meekly sail past and let them go into captivity? Surely the Frenchman with guts enough to sail a privateer out through the British blockade would yearn to re-take those four prizes for the honour of La Belle France?

Fox had bellowed no order for Grey to clap on all sail, to the royals and with studding sails, also, if they could be roused out in time. No sane commanding officer would care to risk studding sails on an unhandy scouse-bucket like this brig. But Fox would, of course, if the necessity of the service required it. . . . He knew Grey was looking at him with that mother-hen expression of proprietal expectancy.

Let the young imp wait!

Again Fox lifted that unlovely voice.

"How does she bear now?"

"Fine on the larboard bow, sir! She's a-coming down to take a look at us, sir, on my oath!"

Fox nodded. He believed Landsdowne. That was what he would do if he commanded a saucy lugger with a turn of speed that would leave the lumbering bulk of *Minion* wallowing.

Very well, then.

If the lugger came down to investigate, he would expect to find anything. He would already know that the English vessel was a brig, the moment he raised her hull he might guess she was a gun vessel and armed with thirty-two pounder carronades. *Minion* was painted Channel fashion, and not in Nelson's chequerboard. He could hope that the Frenchman might not realise the size of his gunports. They were all firmly triced up—aye, and caulked with oakum, too,—from riding out the recent gale. There was a chance. An almost even chance.

And still Grey was looking at him with the air, now, of a constipated he-goat.

An amusing speculation crossed Fox's mind, leading him to wonder just how long Watson would be able to keep silent. Grey, of course, who after all did know something of his curious barnacled commanding officer, would know better than to question what Fox was about.

There was, and damnable it was, to be sure, this business of his handful of men for a crew. Already Grey had proved how fine a seaman he was by handling the brig with so few hands. Handling more canvas now, Grey might think, would only cause monumental headaches when they came to fight the Frenchmen. Fox gained no enjoyment from the thought that if that was so then he was still two jumps ahead of his first lieutenant.

Again he looked at the four prizes. He worked out their subtended angles with no real calculation; he could see the positions as though they were spread out upon some monstrous chess board. He half-turned so as to be able to favour Mr. Midshipman Gruber with a ferocious scowl.

"Make to the prizes, Mr. Gruber. Proceed to the islands. I will join you as soon as possible. Use the signal book intelligently, Mr. Gruber, and make it fast."

"Aye aye, sir," said Gruber. The squeak was noticeably absent from his voice; but he threw himself into the work with an abandon that spoke eloquently of the lad's feelings.

"Mr. Grey," said Fox in the curious icy and yet furiously active voice of his. "I'll have the fore tops'l yard lowered in the slings and the yard braced back."

"Sir! I beg leave to point out that will—"

Mr. Watson leaped as though goaded by a red-hot iron.

"I know, Mr. Watson," said Fox in his devilish way. "It'll look an unholy mess. A real cow's nest. Just make sure, Mr. Watson, that nothing carries away!"

Mr. Watson swallowed. "Aye, aye, sir." He was the master of the vessel; he began to suspect a more complete master inhabited the chunky formidable form of this evilly pugnacious Commander Fox.

As the hands raced aloft and the sail began to behave in ways that would turn any sea-officer green, Fox watched what was happening to *Minion*. Ease her," he growled at the helmsman. Able Seaman Protheroe at the tiller let the massive beam edge across until Fox grunted: "Meet her. Keep her so."

"Aye aye, sir," said Protheroe, feeling all the rush of the vessel in the timbers, wondering what the hell that black bastard Fox was up to now.

Minion had been built in the Rotherhithe yards of Randall and Brent, a place and area of which Fox had particular knowledge, and she was as aggressively British in appearance as any bulldog. The task of running up a tricolour wouldn't be worth the effort. The lugger's captain wouldn't be fooled for a second and, what was more, the act would confirm that the English gun vessel was attempting to trick him. Fox would hoist his own brand of tricolour.

With a speed that told of the freshness of the breeze as much as the fine lines of the chassee maree, the lugger's sails and then her hull appeared over the horizon. Now Fox could comfortably secure all the various calculations in his mind from observations made from the quarterdeck by himself. That was always a most satisfactory condition.

Minion must look a mess. Fox cracked out a further series of technicalities which resulted in further artful disarray in *Minion*'s canvas. She began to be difficult to handle, and Protheroe at the tiller bunched his muscles. Fox sent Tarpy across to help. He daren't push the unhandy vessel too far into disobedience. She was far too much like a recalcitrant donkey at the best of times. Her leeway was now revolting to a captain who liked to feel the stiff heel of a ship to the wind.

Watson kept glancing balefully at Fox—more like pleas from nuns about to be shown the facts of life by Bonaparte's grenadiers, than a sailor's concern for his ship.

"If *Minion* doesn't look like a ship that's in trouble, Mr. Grey, I hope never to sail in one half as bad-looking."

"She does look like a sow's backside, sir," said Grey, with exquisite politeness. "I'll wager Jean Crapaud's chuckling to himself now. He's thinking he's got us dead to rights."

Fox, certainly, wouldn't find too much fault with a French skipper who assumed *Minion* to be in a bad way after the gale. Now if only the bastard would come down within range! If the lugger held off, he'd sail rings around the unhandy brig, keep out of range of the corronades, and blow *Minion* to kindling.

Everyone appeared to be holding their breaths. The lugger held on. Grey sprang up into the shrouds, swinging out, one foot on the ratlines.

"I think she's taken the hook, sir! She's coming down devilish fast!"

With *Minion* disabled and out of the fight, the prizes would fall to the Frenchman like overripe fruit.

"She's coming in!" yelled Grey. "Here she comes!"

"Thank God!" said G. A. Fox. "We've got the Froggy!"

CHAPTER ELEVEN

COMMANDER FOX knew well enought that any captain of one of His Britannic Majesty's ships might make as many mistakes as he liked. If the results of the mistakes could be turned to advantage, the turn of events so contrived as to nullify the mistake and render the operation successful, then all might be well. But only one mistake need be made that turned out unsuccessfully, one single tiny mistake, and that ship's captain would never again be meaningfully employed.

A single mistake would irrevocably ruin a lifetime's career.

This was the spectre hovering balefully at every captain's elbow.

Fox knew all about that.

This, too, was another and sinisterly subtle cause for the famous mad captains of the Royal Navy.

So Fox was a commander at long long last. Life in His Britannic Majesty's Navy remained just as hard and remorseless. He had to fight twice as hard to hold on to his position as a sea-going officer—there were plenty of good men rotting on the beach—and three times as hard to gain any advancement and so be made post. Security for his family by the Thames had always been his guiding principle in life, the Pole Star of his ambition. Only for some great and all-consuming force outside of himself could George Abercrombie Fox have stomached the insults, the slights, the hurts, of his naval career. He had achieved much without recognition; that was common enough. He was not a naval officer of distinction. Distinction was a state reserved for others more favoured. Distinction, and swords of honour, and orders, these were things the cream of the Navy acquired as though by right.

Even then, as Fox let his command take on the appearance of a washerwoman's tub, the tiny tremble of a thought occurred to him—Lloyd's surely ought to hand out a fifty pound sword to the first lieutenant of the flagship in the successful Cloughton's Action? Even if the tangible rewards had been few, undeniably, Cloughton had not lost his battle.

"She's up to something sir!" yelled Grey, and Fox was instantly aware of everything going on around him.

"Bigod! So the bastard is!"

"It's the prizes!" said Mr. Watson, with a full plumpness of his speech which infuriated Grey, at the least. Fox saw the byplay even as he saw success swinging wildly away from his gamble.

The lugger had turned and gone haring for the nearest coaster.

The bastard was going to cut out the prizes and leave poor wallowing *Minion* suffocated by her own inefficiency.

And he could do it, too!

A string of orders ripped from Fox. He yelled and bellowed and long before Mr. Grey could repeat the orders through his trumpet the hands were racing aloft like scalded cats. The yards braced around hard, the topsails sheeted home, the topgallants came out with a great fluttering and were likewise sheeted and braced. *Minion* began to pick up way.

Fox stared through his right eye at the lugger. His left eye might as well be in Chatham for all the good it was doing him.

His furious mind worked out the times and the courses with maniacal speed. No more canvas—that would be the Devil's own work to set and hand. He wanted his men at the guns! Bigod, yes! He wanted those hungry great carronades of his to be fully manned and filled with the same kind of venom animating their master and commander.

"We'll catch him, sir!" bellowed Grey. "Just!"

Minion leaped and pitched over the sea. The wind tore across the deck. Everyone was buoyed up, excited, filled with the tearing excitement of rushing headlong into action.

Spray burst tumultuously under *Minion*'s forefoot. A smother of foam leaped high, curving and tumbling, and for an instant of uncanny beauty Fox glimpsed a rainbow form and gleam and dissolve. *Minion* hurled on over the sea, roaring on, all her canvas taut, drumming, the rigging shrilling, raging on to smash herself in flame and smoke and iron against England's foes.

What that lugger captain must think drove a bleak shaft of amusement through Fox. Fox knew what men thought of him. Old Andy, master of *Caltrop,* had called Fox the toughest bastard on the high seas. That had been when *Minion* was in for refit. Andy had been as tough and spectacular a character as one would wish to avoid down a shadowy Portsmouth side alley. Fox licked his lips. Moments like this, roaring down into action, were the times to prove a man's toughness.

"She's luffing" bellowed Grey. He was wild with excitement, his classically perfect profile struck like an eagle's against the sun shimmer off the sea. "She don't like it!"

The lugger was turning and *Minion* was belting along, every moment bringing her nearer to the point where the range of her carronades would count. There was no longer any need to fool the Frenchman. Fox ripped the necessary orders with a lively sense of acting perfectly in character, of at last getting to grips with some flesh and blood adversary.

"Cast loose your guns!" and "Out tompions!" and "Level your guns!" The caulking would no longer matter. The port lids could be raised and—with a feeling of an inner trembling hunger—Fox realised the impression that would have on the Frenchman. He would see the lines of ports opening and the massive carronades on their slides being run out, like a row of grinning shark's-teeth. Oh, yes, how fine and wonderful and altogether marvellous it was to command a ship of war!

Sergeant Dunn came up, saluting, saying: "Beg pardon, sir. The lady says as she won't go below, sir."

Fox stared at the marine sergeant blankly.

His vessel was cleared for action, the men at quarters, all the necessary preparations made for action and maiming and sudden death. The lady wouldn't go below?

"Take her down, sar'nt! Do what you have to do to make her!"

"Very good sir!" shouted Sergeant Dunn. He bustled off bellowing to two of his marines as he went. Fox couldn't worry his head over the tantrums of a girl with a moustache at times like these. He thrust the inward picture of her long naked legs, the firmness and roundness of her, ruthlessly from his brain. Bigod! He had an action to fight!

These damn chasse maree's were not easy bastards to fight. They were no fish in a barrel. She'd have twenty-four pounder long guns. If he failed to grapple her and do her business fast, she would stand off and pulverise him. And yet, and yet dare he grapple? With his tiny crew?

There had to be a way around this one. He wasn't G. A. Fox if he couldn't sort this one.

A gun banged from the coaster. Fox ricked his lips back.

The lugger's slender hull foreshortened and she leaned so far with the breeze he thought she'd turn turtle. Then she righted and in a weltering smother pranced around to let *Minion* have a taste of her long twenty-four pounders. Her armament for the rest was probably nine pounders. Fox estimated distances, speeds, vectors. He spoke harshly to the men at the tiller and *Minion* came up harder into the wind. She was shuddering and bucking like a recalcitrant colt. He'd colt her! She had to keep this wind for just four minutes more, and then she could be let off, her head swinging away, and Fox might be a little more satisfied. Just four minutes!

The two vessels pounded towards each other, riding the wind, the spray flying, their canvas stiff as boards . . .

Now!

"Port your helm!" bellowed Fox.

Minion reared away to starboard.

"Fire!" said Fox, with great force.

"Fire!" screeched Grey.

The carronades banged off with enormous detonations.

The smoke flew back across the deck, thick and yellow-brown and choking, bringing with it that impossibly exhilarating smell of fired gunpowder. The men were working at their pieces like maniacs. Gruber was yelling them on. Worm, sponge, load with powder, load with shot, ram. The gun captain stabbing down to pierce the cartridge, priming wtih fine grain from the regulation horn, cocking his lock. Grey stared along the line of carronades. *Minion* had swung back under her helm.

This had to be done nip and tuck.

"Fire!" screamed Grey and before the smashing concussions had died he was yelling the men away from the carronades and to the braces. The yards swung. The helm went over. *Minion* tacked like some lamefooted duck; but she tacked and Grey got her around, and Fox was glaring at the lugger and seeing the ballooning puffs of smoke from her side. Where her first broadside had gone he had no idea. He heard a whickering smash and lines parted aloft and blocks spattered down.

MacMillan would have to do deal with that. The brig still handled and sailed. Nothing vital had been shot away, then.

Something was wrong with the lugger, though. Her speed was slackening. Her canvas looked peculiar. As Fox watched so her vast mainsail appeared to change its geometry. The spars buckled. The sail collapsed. It fluttered free for a moment and then fell and enveloped all the forward part of the lugger. The men set up a yell. But *Minion* was surging past again and there was only time to herd them back to the carronades. Fox bellowed at the nearest and sent them scuttling. Again the carronades boomed. The lugger took punishment. Now her captain knew how foolish he had been to allow himself to become entangled with this small but lethal spitfire.

The French flag still flew. Some guns were still firing from the lugger. Fox could not yet order a cease fire. The men threw themselves into reloading. Back they raced. What with handling the vessel and working her battery, Fox had to sort out where the men must be from one minute to the next. The lugger fired again: A single twenty-four pounder, just as *Minion* let rip with her eight thirty-two pounder carronades. It was strictly a "no contest".

Fox saw the lugger's side sprout long whirling slivers of yellow wood. He saw the bulwarks smashed in. He saw the whole after part swept as though by an iron broom.

And, also, he saw *Minion*'s foremast sway, and bend, and collapse, and saw his bowsprit rear and then sag and break. With a most hideous smash fore topgallant, fore top and fore top mast and the bowsprit and jib-boom crumpled into devastating destruction, trailing in lunatic impossibility over his starboard bow.

"Goddammit to hell and gone!" raved G. A. Fox.

Before anyone else could say what they thought, even as Lieutenant Grey ripped up an axe and started for the raffle, that loss of control swung *Minion* sharply. Gun vessel and lugger, they came together, lurching into each other like a couple of drunks outside the Stag and Hounds. The noise of shrieking timber as the hulls ground together created the most devilish counterpoint to the shrieks and the screams.

There was not a second to lose.

Fox tore out his cutlass.

He waved it at the men around him on the quarter-deck . . .

"Come on, you heaping pile of blagskites! We've got to take the Froggy! Come on!" And then he bellowed the words forward, along the deck, so that there could be no possibility of mistake.

"Boarders Away."

It was madness. Sheer lunacy. Everyone knew these French luggers arried enormous crews for their size.

131

But Fox had not failed to observe the thick trails of blood seeping from the scuppers. He knew what his carronades would have done to the deck of the luckless Frenchman. With a quick and savagely determined rush the English could take the lugger. By rapid and ruthless effrontery, they could cow and subdue the French. Bigod! Weren't they doing it all the time? Hadn't Fox done it himself? Well, then, come on, you skyving bastards, come on! Boarders Away!

The mad rush of maniacs who followed Fox would have put the fear of God into the devil himself. They gushed on to the lugger's deck, among the shambles of wounded and screaming French sailors, the raffles of wreckage, the overturned nine pounders. All forward was still smothered by the collapsed canvas, for all her sticks had gone. Fox came in over the quarter and instantly was hard at work bashing in the heads of obstinate Froggies who wanted to contest ownership of their own ship with him. His pistol bang-banged, he brought the heavy muzzle down on the head of an officer, stretched him on the deck. Tredowan was there; but Fox screeched at him to get on with it on his own account. Grey's elegant pistols cracked out and two rushing sailors span and toppled. The evil sound of steel on steel clanged and rang. Men were yelling incoherently now, caught up in the red blaze of hand to hand combat.

Sergeant Dunn's marines shot with the cool professionalism Fox expected of them, and then their bayonets twinkled in cross-play with half-pikes. The first savage rush carried all the lugger's aft sections. A few Frenchmen ran forrard and dived beneath the tangling canvas.

"If they don't come out with their hands up, shoot the bastards!" bellowed Fox.

He glared around, his breathing was only slightly faster than normal, both his eyes were functioning perfectly. He could see the situation clearly.

The whole thing had been quick. Had it not been he would have failed.

Something was going on forward beyond that infuriating raffle of wreckage. Granted there were plenty more Frenchmen still alive, Fox wasn't going to order his men in among that raffle. He grabbed Mr. Smith as that worthy, a cutlass which dripped blood clenched in his fist, hallooed and tried to push past to rush the bows.

"Turn a nine pounder on 'em, Mr. Smith! Cheerly, now!"

The gunner looked at him blankly for a moment, caught up in the lust of fighting. This was quite a change for him, battling away up here in the open air instead of being stuck away down below in the magazines behind his baize screens, surrounded by powder. Then his eyes cleared.

"Aye aye, sir. 'Twill be a pleasure"

In a twinkling a nine-pounder had been spiked around and loaded. Fox yelled angrily to clear men away from the cascable. Without tackle rigged the gun was going to recoil the devil of a long way. But Fox wanted just one good smacking shot of grape.

"Fire!" He spat the word with relish.

The nine pounder cracked out. The trucks squealed in the din and the gun smashed backwards. The smoke shot forward—and in that smoke flew the unpleasant iron balls of grape. The canvas writhed. A spar flew up, scattering chips. Someone up there screamed like a banshee.

"And again, lads!" yelled Mr. Smith, filled now with

133

a kind of proselytizing zeal to teach these poor snail-eating Frogs a lesson or three. "Run her up, cheerly!"

Fox could leave him to it. There were new and ugly developments awaiting his attention.

He ran back to *Minion's* quarterdeck to be clear of the smoke. He had caught a fleeting glimpse out there and if what he had seen was real, he had committed an unforgivable blunder.

As Mr. Smith let off his second helping of grape, a splash forward and a scrambling told of the French launching a boat. They were only too anxious to get clear of their own ship. The lugger was no longer theirs. But Fox stared in a mood that tormented him with his own slackness and incompetence at the sleek form of the French corvette that moved with a sure purpose over the waves towards *Minion* and the lugger.

The nine-pounder went off again. Only a few shrieks followed the concussion. Mr. Grey was yelling the men forrard. Well, they'd taken the lugger. But of what use was that? Here they were, with no foremast and no bowsprit, stuck alongside a shattered lugger, and a smart and lethal corvette was sniffing at their quarters and luffing up to pour in a broadside that would rake them from breakfast time to Christmas Day.

"Light along there!" bellowed Fox. He wasn't going to let some confounded cheeky corvette captain take his whacks at him without doing something in reply. "Light along right cheerly there, you pack of numb-skulls! Stand to your guns!"

Sergeant Dunn and his marines were clearing away the rest of the raffle forrard on the lugger. Here came the hands, leaping the gap between the two vessels, the small amount of tumble home and the lugger's lines making that not too difficult a task.

"She'll be on us!" Mr. Watson was saying. He was

staring at the corvette with a face filled with loathing. "We'll never tear free o' the lugger in time!"

"Of course we won't, Mr. Watson!"

The corvette foamed towards them. Armed with something like twenty twelve-pounders, fast, well-manned, she would blow poor old *Minion* out of the water.

"Of course we can't turn *Minion*. But we can turn her the other way with the sweeps! Mr. MacMillan! Sweeps!" Fox bellowed his orders. "Turn the whole shebang! Put your lollygagging backs into it, you heap o' blagskites! *Pull!*"

Well, it was a chance. A hundred to one—but a chance.

They got the enormously sluggish mass of the two entangled ships almost around in time. Almost they turned them so that *Minion* presented not her vulnerable stern or quarter to the Frenchman but the massive might of her broadside.

Almost, they turned in time . . .

The Frenchman saw what they were trying to do. The corvette's yards braced around only a fraction, her helm must have been put over only a fraction, also; but the combination of those fractions meant she would shoot along out of the arc of fire from the gun-vessel's broadside.

"Goddamitt!" bellowed Fox.

There was absolutely nothing he could do now but wait to receive the corvette's broadside.

The boat from the lugger came into view, low in the water, paddling clumsily with five oars. Later on the corvette could afford to stop to pick up the survivors; now she was hungrily busy about shooting an English vessel to pieces.

The twelve-pounders banged.

135

Fox waited in a petrified certainty that disaster had struck.

The roundshot tore in.

He felt the deck leap beneath him. The main top-mast fell to pitch overside trailing snaking lines that would snatch a man off his feet if they caught him. He saw the larboard aft carronade lurch and heard the deep cathedral gong-note. No one was hurt. He had only a few men left to him after the depredations of Lord Lymm; there were not many human targets for the iron roundshot.

"We're still here!" snarled Fox. "And, bigod, we'll still be here when that snail-eater's rotting on the bottom!"

Here came Mr. Shayne the carpenter with a face as long as a fiddle.

"Well, Mr. Shayne?"

The corvette was swinging, a beautiful sight, curving with bellying sails to come in and smash him again.

"We'm been holed below, sir, well and truly. A foot'n more in the well and rising."

"Be damned to it!"

Fox gazed around as they waited for the next slogging broadside to come in. He felt curiously light-headed. Here he was, a real commander, on his own quarterdeck, in action against an enemy corvette, even if he couldn't bring any of his own guns to bear for the moment, and his damned vessel was sinking under him.

Bigod! He, G. A. Fox, was about to lose his command.

The thoughts that provoked aroused pungent emotions in a man, by God, they did!

Whilst Fox drove his men on to free *Minion* from the entangling and entrapping mass of wreckage binding them to the lugger, the corvette stormed past three

136

more times, and each time punched in a whole concentrated broadside. Three times those twelve-pounders flung their iron shot at the fragile scantlings of the brig.

"She won't stand this kind of punishment much longer, sir," observed Mr. Watson. In the midst of battle with roundshot flying about his ears, the master had achieved a noteworthy calmness. His fussiness dropped from him like the shed skin of a snake. "It's a toss up whether she'll sink first or be blown to bits."

"An interesting wager," said Fox, making his own harsh voice as unemotional as Mr. Watson's. "The calculations of odds should prove most intriguing."

The corvette let fly again and a chunk of wood, a deadly splinter four feet long, whirred between the two men.

"I'd need more figures for an exact calculation, sir," said Mr. Watson, staring reflectively at *Minion*'s main mast which swayed with a sawing dolorous groaning. "If the mainmast comes down—"

"If the mainmast comes down, Mr. Watson, first, step from under, and, two we will carry on with the sweeps."

"Oh, aye aye, sir. I never doubted that for a second."

There was a sensible movement of the vessel beneath him, a kind of sliding surging roll, muffled as to directness; but there, unmistakably there. And here came little Pettigrew, his fair hair already black with powder smoke, his face like a chimney sweep's.

"Please, sir, fust lootenan's comlimens, sir, and we'm free!"

"Thank you, lad."

The harum-scarum little powder monkey stood there, knuckling his forehead, a black scarecrow, ready to run off on his bare feet. Fox heard the splintering groan and looked up. He saw the mainmast swelling. He thought of Mr. Midshipman Lafferty when the old *Henrietta* fought the eighty gun ship of the line, *Saint Lunaire*. The mainmast leaned towards him as though seeking to embrace him.

"Stand you clear, Mr. Watson!" rapped Fox.

He grabbed up little Pettigrew, seized the nipper in his own hard and muscular arms, dragged him aside. The whole enormous bulk of the main mast splintered down, ringing and raging, boomed against the deck and bounced. It bounced six feet, and rolled, and Fox held the powder monkey to his chest and pressed his fair curls with one hand. He glared over the lad's powder-blackened head at the mast. It rolled. It rolled away from them, rolling and twisting, spearing up a sudden fountain of yellow splinters. It rolled away to hang all sloshing and ugly over the far side of *Minion*.

Fox could let out his breath.

He set Pettigrew down on his feet again.

"Are you all right, sir?" came Watson's anxious shout.

"Yes, Mr. Watson, thankee. And so is the younker. Run along, lad, and my compliments to the first lieutenant, and its the sweeps for us!"

"Aye aye, sir." Pettigrew gazed about at the wreckage, and the sudden and awful transition from a familiar main mast that stood like the rod of Aaron all day in the ship, to this monstrous great mass of timber, smashing so frighteningly down around them. He swallowed. He knuckled his forehead and said, again: "Aye aye, sir."

For a powder monkey that was loquaciousness indeed.

Here was Grey, as black and grimed and ripped as young Pettigrew.

"We're free all right, sir. But I'm afraid we've only

three sweeps serviceable." Grey looked devilish. "The others are all smashed."

If there was one thing Fox felt reasonably certain of it was that Lionel Grey was not afraid. Oh, certainly, he was scared silly like them all if he stopped to think; but there was no time to think, and however scared he might be, Grey would never show for a single instant any signs of fear. It wasn't in that peculiar code he adhered to.

"Here comes that back bastard again!" howled Midshipman Felix Gruber.

It was on the tip of Fox's tongue to reprimand the youngster for his shocking language.

Everybody was acting as though this was Armageddon instead of a lousy little scrap with a lugger and a corvette. The corvette captain must be laughing fit to bust a gut. That was what Fox would have liked to do to him. *Minion* was a gun vessel designed to creep into shoal waters and sniff out adversaries. She was not designed for this kind of work, being harried and chased and shot up at long range by a nippy little ship who surpassed *Minion* in every possible way except in the actual weight of broadside. And, of course, the calibre of the crews . . .

"I'll be much obliged, Mr. Grey, if you would kindly place what sweeps you have in the starboard foremost oar ports. I think three men a sweep might serve."

"Star board, sir?"

"Yes, Mr. Grey." Fox wasn't prepared to cut his first lieutenant down to size before others and in these circumstances. "We'll take his next offering as the Good Lord sees fit to send it to us, then we'll kick his guts in for him."

"Aye aye, sir." Grey went off to see about the sweeps.

Fox glared at the corvette. He had his right eye, all shipshape and Bristol fashion.

If anything else went wrong that would fold up its tents, and depart, like that queasy bunch in the Good Book.

Someone yelled up forrard. Grey was cursing and blinding up there. The sweeps were beginning to flail.

The corvette abruptly backed her main topsail. She was going to fetch up near enough alongside their larboard quarter. The lugger had drifted off, now, after Grey and MacMillan had worked like furies to clear her. The corvette captain was going to sit there and calmly pound *Minion* until not one timber adhered to another, until the gun vessel turned into a mere mass of floating debris upon the indifferent surface of the sea.

The breeze had considerably moderated during the action; that flukey compass-quartering wind would begin almost any minute now.

Fox watched the corvette. She looked absolutely splendid. He could see the wink of gold lace on her quarterdeck. Her guns were all run out, pointing at *Minion*. Fox gazed calmly.

A little silence dropped.

Someone was shouting from the corvette.

"Englishman! Surrender! Do you surrender? Haul down your colours, Englishman!"

Partridge had bent on a new ensign to a jury-rigged staff.

Fox did not reply. The sweeps were pulling. Everyone apart from the men at the sweeps and Grey was looking at him.

"Strike, Englishman! You have fought well! Strike!"

Fox jumped on to the wreck of the shrouds where they clumped over the channel, blocks and deadeyes

140

making a kind of platform. "Strike be damned!" he bellowed.

"Better for you to surrender. If you do not strike we will have to finish you. Strike or die, Englishman!"

CHAPTER TWELVE

GEORGE ABERCROMBIE FOX knew all about being called on to strike.

That old felucca, away there in the Mediterranean, and the French corvette, very like this one here and now; oh yes, George Abercrombie Fox had had a taste of being requested by an enemy to strike. He knew his lips must be curling back from his teeth in that expression that could mesmerize the stoutest heart. He knew he must look a devil.

"You'll have to sink me first, you snail-eating bastard!"

"English swine! It will be a pleasure the most intense."

Fox finished this interesting little discourse with a few intriguing suggestions as to what the Frenchman might do with various portions of his anatomy and pointed suggestions as to the probable ancestry of the Frenchman and all his crew.

All the time he shouted his jolly obscenities he could feel the gun vessel inching around as Grey and Mac-Millan kept the men at the sweeps to their work. The stern was swinging.

It was!

It must be!

Even the French captain must be able to see that

stealthy movement now. He would see *Minion's* stern narrowing, her quarter broadening and then the narrow line of her gunports opening out, each port abruptly separated from its neighbour by a vertical bar of yellow hull where before all had appeared a single black streak.

Fox redoubled his bellowing.

"If your whoreson mother wants to find your poxed father it's no good looking in the Court of Miracles! Even they wouldn't stoop so low as to admit your blagskie of a father!"

A screech reached him from the corvette's quarterdeck. A puff of smoke billowed and Fox jumped down from the channel raffle and his hat flew off his head. He did not turn around. The musket ball had only barely missed. He yelled.

"Get my hat!"

But the byplay had given his command those vital few moments. A sudden activity began on the corvette, and Fox saw with evil glee that there was some panic in those frenzied movements. The corvette's yards started to go round. But the wind—ah! the blessed wind!—chose that moment to turn flukey. It died, then puffed from two points backing, then died. It would blow again at any moment; but *Minion* was turning as those men put all their muscles and all their weight into hauling the sweeps. *Minion* turned. Midshipman Gruber yelled.

"When they bear, Mr. Gruber! Not a moment before, mark you!"

"Aye aye, sir!"

Minion turned and her awful broadside opened upon the corvette and Gruber judged it nicely and the carronades lashed out with enormous bellows of sound and billows of smoke.

"Pour it in!" yelled Fox.

The carronades could be trained around far further than a trucked gun and Gruber, putting to good use all the lessons Fox had given him, had them around as far as they would go. The brig shook with the discharges. Fox stared hungrily at the corvette. Smoke gushed and stung his eyes, and then blew away.

The hands set up a caterwauling cheer.

The corvette had been shrewdly struck.

The wind blew, as Fox had known it would, and the pressure on the corvette's foretopmast brought the whole lot down. It plunged overside in grand style.

"Now bite on that one, Johnny Crapaud!" said G. A. Fox.

Mr. Shayne the carpenter appeared, worried. "She can't last much longer, sir."

"She'll last long enough, Mr. Shayne. I promise you that." Fox glared at the corvette. "By God! Do they think I'll give up my ship without a fight?"

Now corvette and brig were sagging together. Held in a stasis, steady on the sea which calmed so much that it appeared positively smooth, the two vessels were drawn together by some alchemical magic, as two corks in a saucer of water. The hands reloaded like demons. Again the carronades flamed. Nearer and nearer, and the corvette's twelve-pounders were hardly firing at all. Nearer and nearer, and now the side of the corvette was smashed and punched in, as a drunken man might smash in a window. Cruel gaping holes appeared in her hull. Gun ports were knocked together. Her mainmast tottered and fell. The awful power of thirty-two pounders, hurling their masses of iron at relatively slow velocity was being demonstrated in gruesome fashion.

Fox saw the dark tell-tale stains of blood dripping from the scuppers.

If this was what the Navy wanted, this slogging match yardarm to yardarm, then George Abercrombie Fox was the right man to give it to them. Not that *Minion* had any yardarms left, and the only one in the corvette was the crossjack—and that erupted in a shower of splinters as it smashed down across the deck as the mizen fell.

For a lightly-constructed ship like the corvette to be repeatedly struck by massive weapons like the thirty-two pounders, was very much like a boy hitting an egg-shell with a hammer.

The deck of the corvette must be running with blood. Dismembered corpses must be littering every inch of space. Men must be screaming there with their eyes torn out, their guts hanging out, their limbs torn away. Those whose heads had been blown clean off would not be shouting any more.

Fox shouted.

The two vessels touched, bow and quarter. Fox yelled.

"Boarders Away!"

He was the first across.

He hit a blood-slippery deck and two men with half-pikes tried to gut him. He chopped left and thrust right and plunged on. An officer in a fancy uniform was yelling desperately for hands to repel boarders; a man in a blue coat thrust his fancy cutlass at Fox. Fox swept his own blade around and plunged the brand into the man's throat. Tredowan, his black kerchief flying, roared in after Fox. Tarpy, stripped to the waist, bore in after them. Then they were all on the deck after Fox, screeching like a pack of intoxicated devils.

In this rough and tumble with pistols banging and men screeching and the tinker-clanging of steel on steel Fox could expect both his eyes to function. This was a

145

sheer bashing match. Of course he should have had more men. He had refused all ideas of striking his colours. Had his crew been larger to start with he might have allowed his humanitarian instincts to overpower his fierce and dogged reluctance to surrender, but the number of possible casualties had been small, and his decision easier.

Now, the task was formidable, despite the enormous and horrific number of dead and wounded Frenchmen lying about the deck, flung there, bloody and broken, by the power of *Minion's* carronades.

Fox and his skeleton crew fought. The men fought because this was the one sure and blessed way of ridding themselves of all their frustrations. This was the time when they could hack and cut, maim and kill, give vent to all the boil of impossible emotions that dull routine held bottled and in check.

George Abercrombie Fox fought with a maniacal determination not to let the French beat him as well as circumstances had beaten him down. Everything in life hinged on what he did in every minute of every day. It was a thought scarcely able to be borne. He dare not lose. Defeat would be the end. He might be killed, of course, shot through or drowned; but that was not the end of which he was thinking as he hacked and cut, slashed and bellowed and fought, fought . . .

Defeat was unthinkable to G. A. Fox.

But defeat stared him in the face, stark and grinning and gleeing in his downfall.

He caught a chaotic glimpse of little Pettigrew running between the legs of struggling French sailors and cutting them up with an enormous knife he must have filched from the cook's galley.

He saw Mr. Partridge, the only master's mate left to him, fling up his hands. There was nothing of Par-

146

tridge's face at all except a red blotch. On the instant Grey leaped past the falling form of the master's mate and whipped his cutlass through the body of the man who had shot his pistol. Grey used a cutlass, just as did Fox. He ought to have a proper officer's fighting sword. It would be more consonant with his dignity. Fox's thoughts jangled then and for a space it was all cut and thrust, hack and slash, stab and slaughter. He was aware of gripping the blue-striped shirt of a man and pulling him onto his cutlass. He was aware of ducking a sweep from a bloodied blade—whose blood was it, he wondered—and so bringing his own blade back and hacking the fellow's legs from under him. He was aware of Mr. Watson putting a ball through the head of his opposite number on the corvette's quarterdeck. He was aware of many desparate events, all coming to him in a blur of motion and violence and action. He wouldn't have noticed these things had he been an able seaman, or a landman. But the fact remained he was the captain, responsible for the lives of the men under his command.

He waded, it seemed to him in the heightened sensations of the fight, through blood to get to the French captain.

Someone was yelling at his back, and he caught Tredowan's words: "She's going!"

He could spare a quick and final glance for his command.

Minion was sinking.

So that was a court martial.

All his new uniforms! His beloved Molière and Villon! His sea chest! His dunnage! Luckily his five-ball sword was not aboard, for he had pawned that for the few half-pence it would bring. Lord Kintlesham had presented him with the five-ball sword. Lord

147

Kintlesham and Sophy—here he struck off the nose of a French seaman who attempted to run him through with a boarding pike—poor silly fat Sophy who was now so slim and elegant and gorgeous and who considered Commander George Abercrombie Fox to be the biggest boor in the world.

Well, wasn't he bigod?

He chopped a massive man with hair matting his chest and arms, steadily forging for the quarterdeck. *Minion* had gone. This corvette had not much longer to live, either. After that they'd all be in the drink, French and English together.

The captain took a deliberate aim at Fox and fired. Fox saw the priming puff and dived forward, low and hard, and the ball went somewhere. He was at the quarterdeck rail now, for the corvette was built on frigate lines. The noise continued, unceasing, dreadful, shot through with screams and yells. Fox felt the corvette sluggish in the sea and knew she was going. But he wanted to make that damned Frog captain strike his flag first. He wanted to ram his insults down his throat.

Lionel Grey panted at Fox's side. His cutlass dripped. "Damned hot work, sir, egad!"

"Aye, Mr. Grey! We're in for a swim directly."

This was sheer madness, this maniac fight aboard a sinking ship.

Fox glared at the French captain.

He bawled in his French he deliberately thickened into an accent that would affront the Frenchman.

"Strike your colours! Strike!"

"Never, Englishman! Not whilst I live!"

"We can soon attend to that, bigod!" snarled G. A. Fox, and he went on to the quarterdeck as a tiger goes down to the waterhole.

Grey was with him. Tredowan was there, too—and his coxswain was wearing an incredibly filthy, old, battered, bullet-pocked, flat-knapped, sword-cut monstrosity of a hat. Fox was minded to bellow: "Get yourself a decent hat, Tredowan, you rascal."

It was only as Grey shoved up past and ran full tilt at the French captain that Fox realised Tredowan had obeyed his order. Tredowan had picked up his hat when it had been shot off his head, was looking out for his captain's headgear in the only sensible way a man could who needed two hands to fight with. Tredowan was wearing Fox's hat.

"You dog!" roared Fox. But he could not turn back.

Grey was reeling back. Grey's hands were at his face. Grey's fingers parted and thick blood welled through.

And all the blood drained from Fox's face. He felt it drain from his heart.

He saw the French captain lifting his ornate sword again, he saw Grey's blood bright upon the polished blade. He saw Grey's cutlass snapped in half, on the deck. He looked; but he could not believe.

"Grey!" he bellowed.

He leaped. The French captain prepared to strike down this mad English captain as he had struck down the lieutenant whose sword had snapped.

The French captain positioned himself, poised, desperate but vengefully ready to settle for the sinking of his ship.

Fox leaped for him. He gripped the Frenchman by the throat. He got inside the sweep of the captain's blade. He glared madly into the Frenchman's eyes.

"Kill Grey would you, you whoreson bastard!"

Very deliberately, Fox drove his cutlass into the

149

man's guts, below his ribs, driving it in and in and twisting it and shoving and twisting . . .

He withdrew and stepped back.

The Frenchman fell.

Fox kicked him in the face.

"You miserable bastard!"

Tredowan was yelling.

"She's going sir, she's going!"

Murder, mayhem, violence, bestiality. The whole world was a stye.

Grey was staggering about spraying blood.

Fox jumped for him. The corvette lurched. She would be gone in moments now.

"Abandon ship!" bellowed Fox.

He took Grey in his arms and ran for the rail. The water was impossibly near. Men were already swimming. Their heads looked like blobs of seaweed, matted and black.

Just before he jumped, with Lionel Grey cradled to him, Fox took a rapid but comprehensive look around the sea horizon.

He swore. He still had strength left to swear.

Another French corvette, the consort of the one sinking under him, sailed grandly towards them, her canvas drawing in the sun, her colours flying, heeling to that flukey wind.

Grey struggled feebly.

"Hold still, lad."

"I'm—all—right, sir."

"I know you're all right, Mr. Grey. Just hold still!"

That second corvette spelled the end. She was the sister to this hulk sinking. Once this corvette had looked so beautiful it made the heart ache to see. But now Fox did not have a thirty-two pounder carronade gun-vessel under him. Once this wreck had looked like this glorious ship sailing so confidently over the sea to take him to a French prison, if he lived. He would dearly like to serve her as he had served her consort.

Out of the tail of his eye he saw the jagged rocks of the Remplades. One of the coasters, one of the prizes he had been detailed to protect, was beating about down there. Why didn't the idiot clap on all sail and make a run for it?

"My face hurts," said Grey. His voice quavered.

"You'll be all right, Mr. Grey. We'll soon sew you up. Now, hold on to me tightly."

"Yes, Mr. Fox." Grey was back when Fox had been a lieutenant and he a midshipman, back in the old *Raccoon*. "Oh, yes, Foxey, you devil, I'll hold on to you through hell itself."

"You do that," said Fox. It was hard to swallow, to get a breath to hold in his lungs.

He'd muffed it. He'd messed it. His command had been sunk. His men were either killed or swimming in the sea. He had taken the damned corvette, but now she was sinking, too.

And Lionel Grey had been wounded.

The future seemed to Fox, then, to consist of nothing.

A fat zero.

A lean zero.

Nothing.

There was no future.

"Hold on, Mr. Grey. Draw a big breath. We're going for a little swim."

"Aye aye, sir. Anywhere, with you, Foxey, you old devil, anywhere in the whole wide world . . ."

Fox looked at Grey and gripped him with a firm yet gentle clasp. Grey's thoughts were maundering. Perhaps

151

that was the best and only thing for a man to do at a time like this.

Clasping Lionel Grey in his arms, Fox leaped into the sea.